FAKE CALLS OF DESTINY

A FLASHBACK ON A FORTESS OF TRUTH AND ITS FRACTURE

DR HARI BALLABH KUMAR

I dedicate this book to our beloved Guru Dr Abdhoot Baba Shivanand Ji

POOJNIYA BABAJI

Contents

Contents

FOREWORD

In the autumn of our lives, when the relentless passage of time compels us to reflect upon the paths we've trodden, we find ourselves immersed in the bittersweet melodiousness of memory. This tale is about three friends—Raaj, Virendra, and Harish—whose destinies have been irrevocably intertwined since their youth. Their story is one of love and betrayal, ambition and sacrifice, and the haunting shadows of unspoken truths. The diffusion of the true fragrance of love can be sensed in their entangled lives and its sex as well as aesthetic layers of varied densities.

Raaj, now a lawyer of great renown, stands as a pillar of integrity and justice. His life, dedicated to the pursuit of truth and righteousness, is a testament to the strength of character. Yet, beneath the veneer of his success lies a heart burdened with unspoken truths and unresolved grievances. His narrative is not just one of legal triumphs, but of the profound emotional battles that he wages in the quiet solitude of his thoughts.

Virendra, a business tycoon of immense wealth and influence, embodies the relentless pursuit of ambition. He was a smart fellow with pleasing personality and was popular among girls during school days. His cunning , drive and a peculiar body language have propelled him to the zenith of success, but not without crossing numerous ethical boundaries. Virendra's story is a stark reminder of the perils of unchecked ambition and the high cost of achieving one's dreams at the expense of one's soul and the lives of those around him.

Harish, once an officer in LIC, represents the quintessence of sacrifice and loyalty. Throughout their lives, he has stood by Virendra, often at great personal cost. His unwavering support for his friend led him into a labyrinth of deceit and moral compromise. As Harish approaches the end of his life, he struggles with the weight of his past actions, desperately seeking to unburden his soul and clear his name. His incomplete confessions, force him to carry the blame for acts he never committed, a victim of the complications created by his lies.

Interwoven with their lives is a silent yet potent narrative—the hidden dimensions of sexuality within the LGBTQA community. This theme, subtly threading through their interactions and decisions, adds layers of complexity to their story. It is a force that shapes their lives in profound and often unspoken ways, challenging their understanding of love, loyalty, and identity.

As Raaj, Virendra, and Harish confront the spectres of their past, they are forced to face the truths about themselves and each other. Their journey through the shadows of deceit and the light of redemption reveals the intricate framework of human relationships. It is a story that delves deep into the heart of friendship, tested by time and the unyielding trials of life.

This novel is more than a tale of three friends; it is a poignant exploration of the human condition. It is about the sacrifices we make for those we love, the ambition that drives us to great heights and greater falls, and the enduring power of truth and redemption. As you turn the pages, may you find yourself reflecting on the knotty dance of life, where love, loyalty, and the quest for truth lead us through a journey of profound self-discovery.

PREFACE

This book was born out of the quiet contemplations of a life spent in pursuit of truth. I have spent decades studying human nature—watching it unfold in society as a teacher by my profession, where the stark realities of life are laid bare. , as a teacher, I have felt if the child is given practice of speaking the truth without any deviation or manipulation then most of the problems of the world can be sorted out and ultimately the youths will be free from frustrations. It was the journey of three friends I've known for a lifetime—that truly pushed me to reflect on the nature of ambition, sacrifice, and the deep bonds of loyalty and conflict of them with the*truth*. . In fourth grade, I read a story titled "Raksha mei Hatya" in a Hindi book. The story was about two young siblings who had pigeons laying eggs on the ledge of their house. When the children saw the eggs, they noticed they looked dirty, and the grassy nest itself was quite messy. So, in the absence of the pigeons, one day, they carefully cleaned the eggs and tidied up the nest. But when the pigeons returned and saw the changed condition of their home and the eggs, they threw the eggs away resulting in the breakdown of the eggs. This story left a strong impression on my mind, and I feel its influence can be sensed in my writing about Harish and Virendra's story. This novel is the culmination of years of thought, not just as an observer but as a man seeking to understand the tangled complexities of human relationships. The love of my wife for the real *truth* in life is the motivating factor in plotting the story of the novel on the surface of *The Truth*. We have the example of Lord Sri Krishna before us. To support truth and righteousness, he did not even think about the curses he would face in the future and accepted his end at the hands of a hunter.

One key lesson I've learned throughout my teaching journey is that teaching others or giving others lessons is the easiest job in the world, but its true impact lies in how we integrate those lessons into our own lives. This insight may find its way into my fiction.

The story you are about to read is a reflection of my observations, drawn from the lives of three individuals—Raaj, Virendra, and Harish—whose fates are inextricably linked. It is written with the weight of decades behind it, during a time when life's pressing questions loomed large: What does it mean to sacrifice for those we love? How far can one go in the pursuit of ambition without losing one's soul? And how does one seek redemption when the truth has become too entangled with lies?

Virendra's rise to power and wealth as a business tycoon serves as both a warning and an aspiration. His cunning has driven him to extraordinary heights, but his success has come at the cost of crossing lines that most would hesitate to approach. Watching his journey unfold, I saw firsthand the consequences of unchecked ambition—the personal toll it takes, not just on the one who seeks it, but on those who stand by their side. Virendra's story is one of triumph, but also deep moral compromise.

By contrast, Harish's story is one of quiet sacrifice. A former officer with the Life Insurance Corporation of India, Harish spent much of his life standing in Virendra's shadow, supporting his friend at the expense of his peace. His loyalty and devotion, which once seemed noble, eventually drew him into a web of lies and moral ambiguity that became too complex to unravel. Harish's heart carried the weight of these lies in the twilight of his life, though many of the acts he was blamed for were not his own. His journey, too, reminds us how easily love and loyalty can lead us astray, forcing us to compromise the very values we hold dear.

The novel tries its best to describe Harish's perspective of truthfulness in life regarding the changes with time.

Here are his changing perspectives, in sequence, with time:

A. Speaking the truth should not be a hard and first characteristic of a person, truth can be remoulded.

B. There should be flexibility in the behaviour as per the demand of the situation and for the sake of one's benefit.

C. The truth might be neglected and untruth can spoken if it benefits others.

D. Untruth can be spoken to save someone's life only.

E. There is no alternative to the truth as the truth is God (Satyam-Shivam) and it should be our ultimate goal.

Raaj, whose voice guides this story, reflects my search for understanding in a world where truth and justice often clash with the messiness of human emotions. Raaj is not just a lawyer of renown; he is a man who wrestles with his burdens—personal truths that cannot always be spoken, and the unresolved grievances that have shaped him. Through Raaj, I wanted to explore the inner struggles of a man whose public victories mask a heart weighed down by the complex ties of friendship and morality.

This novel also delicately weaves the truth of human life through the theme of sexuality, it tries to convey a message that by speaking a lie for fun someone can even take one's life, as in the case of Shyamali Mazumdar. Its story teaches us a vital lesson that the sexual behaviour of a human never determines its character and personality, particularly within the LGBTQA community. It is a subtle yet essential undercurrent, one that reflects the hidden aspects of identity that so often remain unspoken in our lives. Writing this, I sought to highlight how these unspoken dimensions shape our choices and relationships, often in ways we don't fully recognize.

While writing it, I found myself reflecting deeply on life's greater questions. It was during this time that I began studying the lives and histories of people within the LGBTQA community, who are the greatest truth of society, finding parallels to the personal struggles I had witnessed in the lives of my characters. These insights added a layer of richness to the narrative, challenging the characters' understandings of love, loyalty, and family in unexpected ways.

This book is not merely a story about three men; it is an exploration of the human condition, a meditation on the choices we make, and the delicate balance of ambition, love, and sacrifice. As you read, I hope you find yourself drawn into their world, reflecting on your truths, and contemplating the complexities of the relationships that shape us all.

– Hari Ballabh Kumar

Acknowledgements

I would like to express my heartfelt gratitude to all those who have contributed to the creation and success of this novel, "fake CALLS OF DESTINY." Their support, guidance, and encouragement have been instrumental in bringing this project to fruition.

First and foremost, I would like to thank my beloved family for their unwavering belief in me and their constant support. To my son, Taanish Kumar, a talented author himself, I am deeply grateful for your invaluable assistance, Taanish, throughout this writing journey, your expertise and advice have enriched the pages of this novel, and I am indebted to you for your technical support.

To my wife, Barnali, thank you for being my rock and providing me with the space and encouragement to pursue my passion. Her urge for truth in every aspect of life inspired me to weave the plot of the theme of the novel. Your honesty, the quest for truthfulness, understanding, and sacrifices have been immeasurable, and I am forever grateful for your unwavering love and belief in my abilities.

I would also like to extend my heartfelt appreciation to my mother, Aarti Devi, who watches over me from above. Your presence and guidance continue to inspire me, and I dedicate this book to you with immense love and reverence.

I also pay my gratitude to friends, fellow teachers and well-wishers who have supported me directly or indirectly throughout this writing process. Your encouragement and kind words have fueled my determination to bring this novel to life.

Additionally, I extend my thanks to the publishing team and everyone involved in the production of this book. Your dedication and hard work have played a crucial role in bringing my vision to reality.

Finally, I express my sincere gratitude to the readers. Your interest and support make all the effort worthwhile. I hope that "fake CALLS OF DESTINY" resonates with you and leaves a lasting impression.

Thank you all for being an integral part of this journey. Your contributions have made this novel possible, and I am forever grateful for your presence in my life.

With deepest appreciation
Hari Ballabh Kumar

PROLOGUE

Little Rubbaiya approached Harish one day with a very innocent question, "Dadaji, what is truth? Dadiji always tells me to speak the truth, but how do we speak the truth?"

Harish, who had dedicated his life to seeking the answer to this question, now faced the challenge of explaining it to the young girl.

Remembering the motto of LIC of India, which he had lived by - 'Yogakshemam Vahamyaham', meaning 'Your welfare is our responsibility', taken from the Bhagwat Gita's 9th chapter, he found solace in its deep philosophy. It was a belief that gave him strength and reassurance, a belief in the eternal truth within us.

In his career at LIC, he had been asked to explain the meaning of this motto in a job interview, and he had tried to instil the same faith in the hearts of others, including Virendra.

Over the years, he had pondered the meaning of truth and shared his thoughts at public gatherings. But now, faced with Rubbaiya's innocent question, he sought to simplify his understanding for her. Throughout his life, he held onto the belief that Satyam Shivam Sundaram - truth is God and God is beautiful. He grappled with the timeless question posed by the innocent little girl - how to speak the truth? Wrestling with the duality of truths, one pure and divine, the other artificial and deceptive, he sought to decipher the essence of honesty amidst the complexity of human nature. Like a shimmering oasis in the desert, he navigated through the deceptive mirages of falsehood to unveil the eternal beauty and purity of truth.

He explained, "Truth is the alignment of our thoughts, actions, and intentions with the greater good of others and the natural order created by the divine or nature. It reflects our interconnectedness with the world around us and serves as a guiding light towards a harmonious existence."

As he tried to articulate this concept to Rubbaiya, he reflected on his journey searching for truth. He remembered his belief in Lord Krishna and the lessons he had learned from The Mahabharata, viewing life as a quest for truth.

Rubbaiya listened intently, perhaps not fully grasping the complexity of his words, the dissatisfaction of a child who honestly doesn't know the meaning of *Truth*, was obvious but Harish hoped that his attempt to explain the essence of truth would resonate with her in some way.

I

RAAJ-THE SECRET

I am R...a...a...j- The secret. Today I wish to throw light on my own life.

People in different languages call me with different names. In Persian, people call me' Raaj,' in Spanish, 'Secreto', in English and French I am, 'Secret', Chinese call me 'Mimi'. In Russia, I am 'Sekret, with love, in Japan I am 'Himitsu', in Italy I am Segreto, in South Korea -people call me,' Bimil', in Turkey I am 'Siir'. 'Geheim,' is my lovely name in Netherland, in Hindustan I am called ,'Rahasya.'...and so on. By whatever name, people call me but they love me a lot and they wish to have me in their lives. I am not confined within the limits of boundaries of truth and falsehood. I see myself as a vital force within the world, embodying the tension between concealment and revelation. I would view my role with a sense of solemn duty and profound respect for the impact I have on individuals and society. I definitely would understand that my existence adds depth and complexity to life, making me a fundamental aspect of the human experience. My introspection would reveal a character deeply committed to preserving the delicate balance between what is known and what remains hidden, believing that this balance is essential for growth, trust, and the beauty of the unknown. I am a keeper of Depths. I would see myself as the guardian of hidden depths, both my own and those of others. I would take pride in my ability to hold onto truths that are not ready to be revealed, understanding that some things are best left unsaid until the right moment. (For example; every adult knows the mechanism of its birth but it is kept a secret for many years of childhood, revealing this fact at an early age might have ill effects on one's personality.) I am a puzzle of Contradictions. I would recognize that I embody a paradox. On one hand, I thrive on concealment and mystery, yet I also understand the eventual necessity of revelation. This dual nature would be a source of both strength and internal conflict. I am also a catalyst for change or transformation. I would understand that my presence can compel people to introspect, confront hidden truths, and ultimately grow from these experiences. I am a silent protector too as I safeguard information that could harm or unsettle if prematurely disclosed. I take this responsibility seriously, feeling a duty to protect the delicate balance of personal and social harmony. I am an Enigma to be respected . I would feel that the mysteries I harbour are essential for maintaining the allure and complexity of life. By remaining elusive, they contribute to the richness of human experience. I would take pride in being a trusted confidant. I would feel honoured that people choose to confide in them, and they would see this as a testament to their reliability and integrity. They would cherish the trust placed in them and feel a deep sense of responsibility to honour it. I would recognize my role in sparking intrigue and reflection in others. I would see myself as a mirror, reflecting the fears, hopes, and unresolved issues that people might need to address. This reflective quality would be something they value highly. My belief is always in the intrinsic value of mystery. I think that not everything needs to be known or understood immediately and that there is beauty in the unknown. This belief would shape my understanding of self-worth, as I am a crucial element in preserving this beauty. While valuing mystery, I also acknowledge that my worth is balanced by moments of revelation. This balance between holding and sharing would be central to their identity. I hold a deep appreciation for timing. It is my firm belief that the right moment for disclosure is often as important as my existence. Understanding the art of timing would be a cornerstone of my philosophy, guiding their actions and decisions.

It is known that boundaries are essential for personal and collective well-being. I advocate for the right to privacy and the importance of respecting others' limits.

Oh no! I am sorry. I got extremely emotional for my name, which derailed me. I am Rajesh Mathur. My parents called me with a nickname as 'Raj' in my childhood, meaning the Hindi word 'RAJ 'is king for some contexts and kingdom for others, now I am popularly known as' Raaj.'.......Advocate Raaj. I changed in my name from 'Raj' to 'Raaj' only due to my friend Harish Raajdan, although naming alteration was not in fashion in those days. If the Hindi meaning of the surname of Harish is analysed, it comes to be,' the donor of secrets,' Whenever I think of the meaning of the surname of Harish as described by him I recall a dreadful dream cum nightmare of him which he has described for many times. He often used to see a dream at night from his childhood, and whenever I remember, my whole body shudders. *In his dream, it is nighttime, and dark, and a train passes through a tunnel. The rail track is curved and winding, the train is powered by a steam engine, and the area is completely deserted. As the train emerges from the tunnel, its whistle can be heard loudly. Ahead, there is a small halt where a lineman, wearing a blanket, half asleep, stands holding a lantern-signal device. As the train approaches, the tracks ahead are broken, but the signalman, in his half-sleep, shows a green signal instead of red, causing the train to have an accident. Harish wakes up screaming and sweating after seeing this dream every time, feeling anxious and troubled.* In the pages ahead you will find how names or surnames play an important role in our lives, behaviours and characters, how Harish donated secrets and how did I preserve them. I suppose myself , a good actor. What do lawyers do in court? They're simply acting. When two parties are represented in court, one party is right, and the other is wrong. Often, the wrong party manipulates some evidence and wins; sometimes, the right party wins. It all depends on which party's acting is more powerful and convincing, leading the judge to decide in their favor. So, advocacy is entirely an act. Every day, a stage is set where the background remains the same, only the character of the judge's chair seems to change. Yet, the statue of justice stands there with a blindfold and scales in hand, while the characters on the stage change. God has already set a stage for us to act, but when we start playing the role of an actor on this stage of life itself, the chances of complications in life increase. During the journey with me , you might be entangled in the labyrinth of truth and falsehood in the realm of acting on our fabricated stage on the divine stage.

There's a secret I've never shared with my wife Barkha because she would make so much fun of me if she knew. The secret is this: we were three school friends—Harish,

Virendra, and I—who used to participate in our school's Ramayana play during Dussehra. Harish always played the role of Lord Ram, I was always Hanuman, and Virendra would sometimes play Lakshman and sometimes Ravan.

If the life of a human being is segmented into four parts, I am in the third segment but my love for my profession is as dear as Barkha, whose official name is Sushma Mathur, which many of our dear ones don't know.

Please don't mind as I will address my wife by her official name throughout my journey with you.

My love and respect for both my job and my wife are always at its youth.

II
A QUEER CASE

I had a case to plead last year. I still recall its CNR number, it was JHAU018888882023. Known for my expertise in rape cases, as an advocate I had dedicated my life to ensuring that every victim of rape received justice and that rapists faced severe punishments, strong enough to make anyone think thrice before committing such an opprobrious crime. However, this case was different, and my involvement was not by choice but by force or pressure.

Dr Andy, the daughter of the renowned cardiologist Dr. Triveny Kar of Ranchi, was seeking a divorce from her husband, Nitin Saxena, after a year of marriage. The Kar family had secured the services of Shyam Jalani, a lawyer of national fame. Advocate Raaj, i.e. me, was no stranger to high-profile cases, but pleading against Mr Jalani, such a veteran lawyer, added an extra layer of complexity to this already challenging situation.

Despite my unparalleled track record—having pleaded 523 cases, all rape cases, except the first ever case in my career, all won, without taking any fees, earning him a place in the Guinness Book of World Records for his unique contribution to the judiciary system—I, Raaj felt an unusual apprehension about this case. On one hand, I couldn't refuse to take it on, yet it was almost certain that I would lose, risking his impeccable record.

The case revolved around Andy's demand for a divorce from Nitin. There were whispers that Andy was acting under pressure of her parents. The Kar family claimed that Nitin was both asexual and aromantic, grounds for Andy's request for divorce. These claims added layers of complexity to the case, making it an open-and-shut matter in the eyes of many.

I stood in the courtroom, pondering the intricacies of this case. My mission had always been clear—to fight for justice for rape victims and ensure rapists were punished severely. But this was a divorce case, something outside his usual realm of expertise, rape and divorce are at the extremities as parameters of human sexuality, they both are standing at opposite ends of male-female segments. I was in a thought that I couldn't help much in this case but wonder why I had been chosen for this case and what implications it might have for my career and personal mission. My wife Sushma is an intelligent lady I generally discuss the case at night which I had to plead the next day in court but it could not be possible for this case as divorce in the absence of sex, in married life is a taboo in India. My team of lawyers are very efficient at their work and prepare the legalities of the case very sincerely and they study all the pros and cons regarding each and every case still I use the instinct of my wife in the courtroom. But today the situation is different, in general Disputes, personal egos, and extramarital affairs are reasons behind the divorces. As pieces of information collected by my assistants in this case, that Nitin was in a live-in relationship with his colleague Somya for two years when they were working in Infosys, Beguluru office. My assistant Jannie even claims that Somya had given birth to a girl child in Sacred Oak Hospital, Electronic City, Bengaluru. Jannie had enough pieces of evidence for the same from hospital records. Her visit to the apartment, where the couple spent their days during their live-in relationship. It was Gopalan Florenza Apartment, Electronic City, third floor, flat number 304. "During lockdown in the middle of Corona period, both had work from home, sir, I contacted the Singh family in flat number 305, where I got confirmation birth of the child but Sir, Mrs Singh, was trying to hide something, which might be speculated later on. " Jannie explained the fact to me and felt proud that she collected more than enough evidence to prove in the court that Nitin was not asexual, he is simply straight and perfectly normal. I exclaimed, "Jannie...Jannie.., the case is not as simple as you think, yesternight Mr Virendra, Nitin's father as you know, came to me and told me everything which you described right now and gave a strict instruction that the matter of the live-in- relationship with Nitin and Somya should not be revealed at any cost in the court, whatever be the verdict of the case." I worried, "Why does Virendra prefer the disclosure of his son's asexuality to his normality." I told Jannie, "You don't know..Virendra Saxena has been my friend since my school days. He had always been a mysterious guy to me, I could never understand his actual intentions in his activities." " Sir, then the case is becoming complicated with time,... my inner voice says I can do something to get some clue which might give the case some right direction, sir, there is a restaurant named 'Ruposhi Bangla', which is famous for its Bihari, Bengali and Jharkhandi cuisines. It is situated in the crowded locality of Electronic City, the restaurant has a delivery boy whose name is Prakash,.. he is from a small village near Bokaro Steel City, ... he delivers food in many flats of nearby apartments, the best part is that he keeps his ears and eyes open for happening in the lives of most of the apartment dwellers,.. he is famous by the name: of Byomkesh Bakshi, there. " I was surprised," interesting-Byomkesh Bakshi from my native place.". Jannie continued, " Sir I could not meet him as he had gone to his village,... sir, if you request the judge for the next hearing without jumping to some conclusion, my gut feeling says I can have some vital information regarding the case from Byomkesh Bakshi..sorry sir, I mean from Prakash." As the courtroom proceedings began I suddenly came out of thoughts of last night's conversations with Jannie, I prepared myself to face Shyam Jalani, ready to uphold his principles and seek the truth, regardless of the outcome. The stakes were high, not just for the parties involved but also for my legacy. Would I be able to maintain my unblemished record, or would this queer case mark a turning point in my illustrious career? No' instinct' for this case from Sushma's side. Only time would tell the consequences, as the drama unfolded in the hallowed halls of the Ranchi High Court.

III

COURT-ROOM DRAMA

The morning sun streamed through the tall windows of the Ranchi High Court, situated near the HEC Industrial Complex, casting a golden hue across the room. I stood at my table in the courtroom, shuffling through a stack of documents, my mind racing with the complexities of the case I was about to plead. Known for my expertise today, I found myself in unfamiliar territory, in front of Mr Jalani, a seasoned lawyer with a commanding presence, embroiled in a divorce case with unusual apprehension.

Despite my initial reluctance, I had taken on the case, though with an unsettling sense of foreboding. Harish Rajdaan, my friend, had requested over the phone that I plead for this case, and I could not say 'no' to him.

As I pondered the intricacies of the case, the courtroom buzzed with anticipation. My team had gathered substantial evidence to the contrary, indicating that Nitin had been in a live-in relationship with a colleague, Somya, and they had a child together. This fact could be enough to justify in the court that Nitin was straight rather than asexual, but I had been forbidden to reveal the truth about Nitin's normal sexuality.

The courtroom doors opened, and a hush fell over the spectators as Judge Arvind Kumar entered, taking his seat at the bench. I glanced at his assistant, Jannie, who had worked tirelessly to gather evidence for use in court.

I stood up, ready to present my case. Despite an unsettling feeling of unease, I knew that revealing the truth could have severe repercussions. Yet, my principles demanded that I seek the truth, regardless of the outcome. Today, for the first time in my career, I felt like I was swimming against the current of truth.

"Your Honor," I began, "we are here today to address the divorce petition filed by Dr Andy Kar against Mr Nitin Saxena. The grounds for this petition are claims of asexuality and aromanticism on Mr Saxena's part. However, we have substantial evidence that contradicts these claims."

Shyam Jalani, the seasoned lawyer, rose to his feet. "Objection, Your Honor. The claims I presented are unsubstantiated and irrelevant to the case at hand."

Judge Kumar nodded, allowing me to continue. "Your Honor, asexuality in either a male or female is quite subjective, and it does not lead to the suspension of the institution of marriage. Your Honor, I would like to refer to the great Hindu epic, The Mahabharata, which had a character 'Shikhandi' who had a successful married life despite his questionable sexuality."

The courtroom buzzed with murmurs as I presented the documents and testimonies that Jannie had gathered. Despite the compelling evidence, I couldn't reveal the full extent of Nitin's relationship due to Virendra Saxena's insistence.

As the arguments continued, my mind drifted to my conversation with Jannie. She had mentioned a delivery boy named Prakash, known as Byomkesh Bakshi in the local community, who might have vital information. However, Prakash was currently in his native place, and I couldn't rely on him for immediate insights.

A turning point came in the case when Mr Jalani started trembling. The file he was holding shattered on the floor near his table, and he seemed to be pressing the upper part of his chest with both hands. People rushed to his aid, and it became clear that he was experiencing a cardiac arrest. He was immediately taken to Dr. Kar's nursing home for medical treatment.

Judge Kumar addressed the courtroom, calling for order and announcing an adjournment of two hours due to the health emergency of Mr Jalani. The courtroom buzzed with speculation and concern as the proceedings came to a halt.

When the court reconvened, Judge Kumar made a decision that surprised everyone. He ordered that six months be given to the couple to save their marriage, considering the complexities of the case.

As I left the courtroom, a sense of relief washed over me. The verdict provided time to uncover more truths and perhaps find a resolution that upheld justice for all parties involved. However, it also made me realize the importance of delving into taboo subjects like human sexuality, not just for the sake of my case, but for my personal growth and understanding.

As I reflected on the events of the day, I knew that this case would mark a turning point in my career. It opened my eyes to unexplored areas of law and human nature, pushing me to delve deeper into the complexities of human relationships.

In the days that followed, I dedicated myself to learning about the private lives of LGBTQIA+ individuals, seeking to understand their struggles and rights. The recent verdict by a 5-Judge bench of the Supreme Court on petitions seeking marriage equality for the LGBTQIA+ community weighed heavily on my mind, shaping my perspective and driving me to advocate for justice and inclusion in my future cases.

As I delved into these taboo subjects with newfound curiosity and empathy, I knew that this courtroom drama would not only add a special credit to my name but also my journey as a lawyer seeking truth and justice in a world full of complexities and contradictions.

IV
SHIKHANDI-THE WARRIOR

Before going deep into the lives of the third gender I determined to explore our ancient scriptures and came across many characters in Hindu mythology which validifies complexity in human sexuality. Some of them are being penned down. [*Shikhandi is one of the most complex and intriguing characters in the Mahabharata, an ancient Indian epic. His life story is a rich shade of themes including gender identity, fate, duty, and revenge. Shikhandi was originally born as a female named Shikhandini, the daughter of Drupada, the king of Panchala. Shikhandini was the reincarnation of Amba, a princess of Kashi. Amba had a tragic past; she was abducted by Bhishma, an unparalleled warrior of his time, during her swayamvara (a ceremony where a princess chooses her husband from among suitors). Bhishma had intended to marry her off to his half-brother Vichitravirya, but Amba loved Salva, the king of Salva, refused the proposal. Bhishma let her go, but Salva rejected her due to her abduction.*

Amba, humiliated and seeking revenge, undertook severe penance to please Lord Shiva, who granted her the boon that she would be the cause of Bhishma's death in her next life.

Thus, Amba was reborn as Shikhandini, Drupada's daughter. Even as a child, Shikhandini displayed qualities of bravery and valour, typical of a Kshatriya (warrior class). However, her life was marked by the quest to fulfil her previous life's vow to kill Bhishma.

Shikhandini's transformation from female to male is a significant aspect of her story. As she grew older, she became more determined to exact revenge on Bhishma. Her father, King Drupada, supported her but was deeply troubled by the implications of her vow.

In the Mahabharata, it is said that Shikhandini, on the eve of her marriage took a plight to forest, in order to hide her sexual identity , encountered a Yaksha (a nature-spirit) named Sthunakarna in the forest. Moved by her plight, Sthunakarna exchanged his gender with Shikhandini. Thus, Shikhandini became Shikhandi, a man, while the Yaksha took on her female form. This transformation was crucial for Shikhandi's role in the Kurukshetra war, as it enabled her to participate as a male warrior.

Shikhandi played a pivotal role in the Kurukshetra war, primarily due to the prophecy that Bhishma could only be defeated by someone who was born a woman. Knowing this, Krishna and the Pandavas devised a strategy to use Shikhandi against Bhishma.

During the war, Shikhandi rode into battle against Bhishma, with Arjuna using Shikhandi as a shield. Bhishma, bound by his vow not to fight a woman, refrained from attacking Shikhandi. This hesitation allowed Arjuna to shoot arrows at Bhishma, ultimately leading to his fall. Thus, Shikhandi fulfilled the prophecy and Amba's vow, becoming the *cause of Bhishma's downfall.*

Shikhandi's strengths lie not just in physical prowess but also in the resilience of spirit and unwavering determination. From a young age, Shikhandi was imbued with a sense of purpose-driven by a powerful past-life vow. This sense of destiny gave Shikhandi immense inner strength and the courage to face one of the mightiest warriors of the Mahabharata, Bhishma.

As a warrior, Shikhandi was skilled in archery and combat. However, his most significant strength was his role in the strategic narrative of the war. Shikhandi's presence on the battlefield exemplified the use of psychological and moral tactics in warfare, highlighting the importance of vows, curses, and prophecies in the Mahabharata's grand narrative.

Shikhandi's story provides an early exploration of complex gender identities in Indian mythology. Born female, transformed into male, and recognized as such by society and himself, Shikhandi's gender identity is fluid. This fluidity is accepted and even instrumental in the fulfilment of destiny within the epic.

In terms of sexuality, the Mahabharata does not delve deeply into Shikhandi's relationships or desires. The focus remains on his duty, identity, and the overarching narrative of revenge and justice. However, Shikhandi's gender transformation challenges and expands the traditional binary understanding of gender roles in ancient texts.

Shikhandi remains a powerful symbol of courage, determination, and the complex interplay of gender and identity in mythology. His story reminds him of the multifaceted nature of human identity and the timeless struggle for justice and self-realization. In contemporary times, Shikhandi's narrative resonates with discussions around gender fluidity and the recognition of diverse gender identities.

As far as his married life is concerned, there are no such pieces of evidence but some stories of his marriage to the princess of the Dasarna kingdom and having a son named Kshatradeva validate that he was a full-fledged man. In a version of the story, after marrying Shikhandi, the princess of Dasarna discovers Shikhandi's orientation and runs to her father, Hiranyavarna. Insulted by this event, Shikhandi ran away to the forest and was thinking to end his/her life, where he met the Yaksha, who took pity on him and gave her manhood for one night. With Yaksha's manhood, Shikhandi made love to a courtesan sent by his father-in-law and proved that he was no woman. The princess was then forced to return.]

In the courtroom, during my recent case, I gave my justification with an example of Shikhandi's married life and he had children but it had no logic in mind I told it with the anecdotes I came across in my life.

But now I am aware of the fact, from Udyog Parva of Ved Vyas' Mahabharata.

Great dancer Michel Jackson had changed his sex biologically several times with the boon of Medical science and enjoyed the sex life of male as well as female. Initially, I too was not convinced so much but Hindu mythology has pieces of evidence of sex change and the existence of the so-called LGBTQA community.

If all the pieces of evidence collected by Jannie and the team, prove to be an illusion and even Virendra's confession of Nitin's live-in relationship proves to be crafted finally it be established that Nitin was indeed asexual, and this was the root cause of the issues in his marriage. I believed that with proper medical and psychological intervention, their relationship could be salvaged. However, I was unsure about what Nitin's father, Virender, wanted - did he wish for Nitin to remain married to Andy, or did he want their relationship to come to an end? This uncertainty left me feeling lost and confused as to the best course of action for the court case.

V

OTHER LGBTQA THEMES IN MYTHOLOGY

Hindu mythology has stories and characters that reflect a wide spectrum of gender identities and sexual orientations. Though traditional texts rarely speak of homosexuality directly, they often feature gods and mortals undergoing gender changes, engaging in same-sex relationships, or embodying a mix of male and female attributes. These stories can be found in sacred texts like the Vedas, Mahabharata, Ramayana, and Puranas, as well as in regional folklore.

[**Agni,** God of Fire: Agni, the god of fire, is married to the goddess Svaha but also has a male partner, Soma, the moon god. Agni receives Soma's semen in his mouth, paralleling his role in accepting earthly sacrifices. In another myth, Agni swallows the semen of Shiva, which leads to the birth of Karttikeya, a god of beauty and battle, showing divine same-sex interactions.

Justification:

In Hindu mythology, Agni is not just a physical representation of fire, but also symbolizes transformation, purification, and energy. Fire is seen as a purifying force that transforms offerings into a form that can be received by the gods.

The idea of Agni receiving Soma's semen can be seen as a metaphor for the process of transformation and creation. Soma, the moon god, represents the cooling, nurturing energy that balances Agni's fiery nature. By receiving Soma's semen, Agni can channel this energy and use it for creation and sustenance.

Similarly, Agni swallowing Shiva's semen leading to the birth of Karttikeya can be interpreted as a representation of the unity and interconnectedness of all beings. In Hindu philosophy, all of existence is seen as interconnected and interdependent. Through the divine same-sex interactions of Agni and Shiva, the idea of oneness and unity is reinforced.

Overall, these myths can be seen as symbolic representations of deeper philosophical concepts, such as the balance of energies, the process of transformation, and the interconnectedness of all beings. These stories serve to teach important lessons about acceptance, unity, and the cyclical nature of existence. Direct interpretation of such mythological facts may lead us toward fatality.

Mitra and Varuna: These two gods are depicted as intimate friends with deep bonds. They are often shown together and are associated with the ocean's depths and surface. Some texts describe them engaging in same-sex relations, symbolizing their unity.

Justification:

In Hindu mythology, Mitra and Varuna are considered the guardians of the universal order and uphold the concepts of truth, morality, and justice. They are also associated with water, which is seen as a symbol of purification, life, and sustenance. The ocean, with its depth and surface, can be seen as a representation of the complexities of life and existence.

The depiction of Mitra and Varuna as intimate friends with deep bonds emphasizes the idea of unity and cooperation in maintaining cosmic balance. Their same-sex relations can be interpreted as a metaphor for the harmonious blending of opposites, symbolizing the union of complementary forces in the world. In Hindu philosophy, there is a belief in the interconnectedness of all beings and the harmonious coexistence of different energies.

Ardhanarishvara: This deity is a fusion of Shiva and his consort Parvati, representing a half-male and half-female being. This form signifies the unity and balance between genders, embodying the concept of totality beyond duality.

Krishna and Aravan: In Tamil mythology, Krishna transforms into a woman named Mohini to marry the hero Aravan, who wishes to experience love before his sacrificial death. This story is commemorated by the Hijra community in an annual festival where they enact the marriage and mourn Aravan's death.

Vishnu as Mohini: Vishnu, in the form of the enchantress Mohini, attracts Shiva, resulting in the birth of a child. This myth illustrates the fluidity of gender and attraction, showing divine beings embracing both male and female aspects.

Arjuna as Brihannala: In the Mahabharata, Arjuna is cursed to become a member of the third gender. He lives as Brihannala, teaching music and dance, highlighting the acceptance and integration of gender variance.

Ila and Budha: The story of Ila, who alternates between male and female, and Budha, who marries Ila during her female phases, showcases gender fluidity and transformation.

Bahuchara Mata: This goddess is a patron of the Hijra community. Myths tell of her cursing men to become impotent or to adopt female characteristics, enforcing her connection to gender and sexual variance.

Samba: Krishna's son, Samba, dresses as a woman to trick people, and is later cursed to give birth, further linking him to themes of gender fluidity and transformation.

Queens of Maharaja Dilipa: In a Bengali myth, two widowed queens conceive a child together by the blessing of Shiva, showcasing a same-sex relationship leading to procreation.

Ganesha's Birth: The elephant-headed god Ganesha has various origin stories, some of which involve creation from non-procreative bodily fluids, emphasizing the sacredness of diverse forms of birth.

Sangam Literature: Ancient Tamil texts also reference intersex individuals and same-sex love, showing that these concepts have long been part of Indian cultural narratives.]*

Overall, these myths can be seen as symbolic representations of deeper philosophical concepts, such as the balance of energies, the process of transformation, and the interconnectedness of all beings. These stories serve to teach important lessons about acceptance, unity, and the cyclical nature of existence. Direct interpretations of such mythological facts may lead us toward fatality.

In totality, I summarised that Hindu mythology includes numerous instances of gods and mortals engaging in same-sex relationships, undergoing gender changes, and embodying both male and female qualities. But all of them are symbolic and many of them are yet to be decoded. If we directly jump into these stories we may find the fluidity and diversity of gender and sexuality in ancient Indian culture, offering a rich drapery of narratives that resonate, whether really or virtually, with modern understandings of LGBT identities. But I did not find any evidence of queers and asexuals representing Q and A from the present so-called LGBTQA community.

VI
GOD'S CANVAS

Once in my childhood I strolled through the papaya garden with my father, a man of both farming and business acumen, I watched as he instructed Sunder, our household cum farm help. to cut down some of the seemingly healthy papaya trees. Confusion gnawed at me, prompting me to question his decision. "Bapu," I queried, using the endearing term for my father, "why have you ordered the cutting of these lush, green trees that appear to be thriving?" With a knowing smile, he explained, "Raaj, my son, observe the flowers on these trees. They grow in a twisted, vine-like manner, indicating that they will never bear fruit , so they are useless and they will consume the nutrition of the soil." I had become more curious and asked him, "Why it is so, Bapu?" He continued explaining " These trees are neither male nor female, they are special creations of god or might be an err of Him........" Bapu had tried explaining many things about the biology of those trees and the engineering of God but I could not find interest in his explanations as I failed to understand, so vibrations created by his voice could not stimulate my brain ultimately my curiosity faded away on that day. Today, sitting in my study room, I try to recollect my father's voice, the vibration of one word, 'God's special creation' was sending continuous signals in the temporal lobe of my brain. Today I miss my father a lot for listening to him again on this issue, and I got a lesson too, not to ignore your elder's wisdom and experience. " May I come in, sir?' Jannie's voice brought me back from my thoughts. " Yes-yes Jannie, come in, and have a seat." " The Ministry Of Utmost Happiness(Arundhati Roy), Magical Palace(Kunal Mukherjee), The Life Apart(Neel Mukherjee), Yarana: Gay Writing from India (Hoshang Merchant), My Father *Cannot* Be Gay(Devdutt Pattanaik)... sir, what are these? in the place of your law books, " Jannie pointed towards books lying on my table and again continued," Sir, case number no JHAU018888882023, has completely changed your course of life." My lips turned into a parabolic curve of smile for her extraordinary memory. She has extraordinary calibre, at the age of only 26 she can give details of all cases of my firm, S.R.Associates during the last five years. A short-heighted dark-coloured lady, Jannie, with always a sweet smile on her face, is very dear to me, she is just like my daughter. on the very first day of her joining the firm, she asked me," Sir, does your aunty's real name start with 'S'? It surprised me, "How did you come to know, as all of us call her Barkha at home?" " Sir it's so simple to guess, in the name of your firm 'R' is the first letter of your name,... 'S' must be the first letter of your wife's name and 'S' at the beginning of the firm name indicates that you respect her dignity." At that moment of that very day, I was speechless, for many reasons, I was only thanking the angel in the form of a transgender who added her to my life. But at this moment I replied for her innocence," I am just trying to gather information regarding the LGBTQA community, it might be helpful in any case." " Sir, their community is different from ours, but everyone should be concerned about them, Sir, whenever I see transgenders begging in the red lights I become quite emotional as if I have some linking with this community." After this conversation, she drew a law book from the almirah and started searching for something perhaps for some ongoing case of the firm. Her statement regarding her linking to the LGBTQA community, made me think, " The raaj..the secret which I have been hiding for 26 years, is this revealed to her ??" At second thought I consoled myself, how, ..how is it possible? As per my name, Raaj, I have kept many secrets hidden within the dark areas of my heart, and I enjoy it, whether it is the raaj (secret)of my friend Harish or the raaj (secret)of Jannie's birth. I never wish that either Harish or Jannie would come to know that I ever knew their secrets. If you watch a modern piece of artwork by a great painter, the meaning of many of the sketches cannot be found easily or different people's perspectives regarding the artwork may be different. But, the painter knew exactly what he wanted to tell through his strokes. God is the greatest painter, every painting of Him has some special significance we can not understand what message He wants to convey through His act. Every birth of a human being is important and everyone is special, before the birth fertilisation of sperm and ova takes place and in this process the fastest, the healthiest and the best sperm take part so the birth of every human child is the special creation of God and it is true for other living being too, its gender doesn't matter whether male, female or any part of so created the LGBTQA community of humans. At the very time of birth, everyone is pure, innocent, and beautiful. The best creation of the Almighty changes with time depending on, the acts played by one with the growth decide the destiny, society is equally responsible for shaping, deshaping and reshaping the human being. For instance, the so-called LGBTQA community too has some sections which have been formed by human nature, behaviour, situation, emotion and habits. Among the various sections of the LGBTQA, many sections such as queer and asexual do not have much evidence in history. The categories of homosexuals might have situationally formed sects of the so-called community. I always have goosebumps in my body whenever think about the root cause of the deformed personality of my friend Harish. He suffered from some personality disorder till he became a disciple of Avdhoot Baba Dr Shivanand and turned into Shivyogi. Due to him only I too became one of the finest disciples of Avdhoot Baba and a proud Shivyogi today. After our schooling, in the late 80s Harish and I opted for different colleges to join. He was staying in the college hostel, Saraswati Puja, in those days, was one of the most important events in the lives of students of Bihar and West Bengal and later on Jharkhand too. The pooja in the hostel of Harish was very famous and most remarkable in the region. I was invited by Harish and Virendra (as he had joined the same college and hostel after schooling) on this holy occasion. It was a sweet and unforgettable meeting after our schooling. On the day before pooja, everyone was busy with preparations as decorations and other preparations are expected to be the best. Amid all these clamours of celebration Harish and I were sitting in the hostel room. He was as somehow sad and his expression could be read that he wanted to say something but could not do so. I understood his situation as during school life I felt that no one knew Harish better than me. I compelled him to speak out about the forbidden agenda, which was suffocating his heart. In the end, unwillingly, what he told me about his elder brother's conduct towards him, made us cry, tears were uncontrollable from all four eyes there. At that time I could not say sufficient words for consolation as I knew his elder brother very well, he was well-behaved and intelligent. I could feel the real traumatic mental state of my friend, he could not tell about the event in the family as his elder brother was an apple of his parents' eyes, and no one would be ready to believe Harish, his family had been always hypnotised by his success and depressed by the average academic performance of Harish. His elder brother was the top ranker in his medical college whereas Harish had joined an ordinary intermediate college due to his average performance in his secondary board examination. Had I been as good a counsellor then as I think of myself today, my dear friend would not have been the owner of a fractured personality for his important years of career. Today I am enriched by the fact that homosexuality. This instinct or behaviour is completely situation-driven which ultimately one assigns it a "valance". of liking in the amygdala of one's brain and hence one enters this forbidden arena of sexuality.

Mahatma Gandhi and Hermann Kallenbach had a complex and controversial relationship that has been the subject of much speculation and debate. Kallenbach, a German architect and close friend of Gandhi, played a significant role in Gandhi's life and work, particularly during his time in South Africa.

Some historians and biographers have suggested that Gandhi and Kallenbach had a romantic relationship, citing their close emotional bond, the intimate nature of their correspondence, and the fact that they lived together for a while. Others have dismissed these claims as mere speculation, arguing that the relationship between Gandhi and Kallenbach was purely platonic.

The truth about the nature of Gandhi and Kallenbach's relationship remains unclear, as both men have passed away and there is limited evidence to support either side of the argument. However, their friendship was undoubtedly important to both of them, and Kallenbach's support and companionship had a significant impact on Gandhi's life and work.

Regardless of the nature of their relationship, Gandhi and Kallenbach remained close friends until Gandhi died in 1948. Their legacy lives on through their shared commitment to nonviolence, social justice, and the pursuit of truth.

At the time I did not have much pieces of evidence and knowledge to explain and console my friend Harish

Regarding his elder brother, I had been surmising badly for a long but now I have somehow different thoughts that the sexual and private life of one does not determine one's character till it does not impact others. People's character is typically defined by their thoughts, feelings, and actions. It is shaped by a variety of factors, including upbringing, life experiences, personal values, beliefs, and choices made over time. Character can be seen in how a person treats others, handles difficult situations, and stays true to their principles. It is often reflected in honesty, integrity, empathy, and resilience. Ultimately, a person's character reflects who they are as a human being and how they interact with the world around them.

It cannot be denied that when a person's intimate life is brought into the public eye, the narrative can be shaped and reshaped by various individuals, each with their motives and interpretations.

If I think today about the character part of Sarvesh Bhaiya it is unquestionable at that time, the urge of that age is understandable too, but the midnight act with his younger brother who shared a hostel bed with him seems to be a crime to me even today if I see the matter with the lens of law. He is a well-known venereologist in India, today, people worship him for his services. The whole medical fraternity salutes him for his services in South Africa during the outbreak of STDs in 1996. WHO awarded him with the most prestigious Ihsan Dodramaci Family Health Foundation Prize.

About Dr Sarvesh Raaajdan Raajdan as told by Harish:

During his stay in Kei Mouth(South Africa) village, he shared a room with Dr Lethabo, his South African colleague in the ongoing health project. In his letters, bhaiya always spoke highly of Dr. Lethabo, praising, his physique, his body flexibility, his being of American origin, his skills and his dedication to their work together. However, Rajni Bhabhi did not appreciate the emotional language which bhaiya used to describe Dr. Lethabo, questioning why he was so effusive in his praise for his African counterpart. I sensed a hint of insecurity and suspicion in her comments, but I was unsure how to respond to such a sensitive issue. But the situation made me very uncomfortable and I was filled with intoxicating thoughts.

VII

HUSTLES AND BUSTLES OF SARASWATI PUJA

As I have mentioned earlier Harish and Virendra had invited me to their college hostel during the auspicious occasion of Saraswati Puja. Goddess Saraswati is supposed to be the goddess of knowledge. She is associated with wisdom, music, art and learning. Students must worship the goddess but I learned that every aspect of puja can be felt among the students except the devotion. From the collection of money for the celebrations, college students there, in those days had to cross many ordeals. Most of the collections were drawn from transport vehicles, especially trucks, plying through nearby roads. Most of the time the collections were done forcibly not willingly. There were incidents of truck accidents as the drivers tried to escape the overburden of so-called pooja chanda(donations). Throwing stones to speedily plying trucks by students was one of the heinous crimes committed by them in the name collection. The police and administrations didn't take major steps against all these due to political pressure. Politicians support the students in the collection of pooja as they could use the students during elections. Mass arrest of students and their release after a few hours was one of the common dramas played by police as they used to support students. Sometimes students had to face the fake lathi charge of the police. Altogether this celebration of today was an outcome of many risks. A beautiful idol of the goddess with Veena magnifying the attraction of their college hostel pooja pandal, which was placed on a magnificently crafted candle stand. Sudhirda, a great sculptor from Asansol was the mastermind behind the creation of such a divine and graceful statue.

Everyone except Virendra and I had gone to attend a meeting of the College Hostel Pooja Committee for allotment of duties for tomorrow, the main pooja and visharjaan.

Finding me in solace, Virendra began with the love story of Harish, he is a good storyteller indeed.

The love story of Harish told by Virendra,

It was a cold, evening last December when a Harish, reached Court Mor, Dhanbad for a usual visit to the nearby Patliputra Medical College to meet his elder brother, a lavender breeze enveloped him as a man-driven rikshaw crossed. Of a sudden, he shouted, 'Stop, stop,....rikshaw,..rikshaw.' The rickshaw puller stopped the rikshaw at a few furlongs,s, 'Kya huwa babuji , kyon chilla rahe ho (what happened, why are you shouting) ? ' said the rikshaw puller. 'Dekh nahin rahe ho , bhaiya, madam ka dupatta aapke rikshaw ke chain mein phans gaya hai, aap thoda bhi aage jaate to , dupatta ka doosra sira madam ke gardan mein phans jaata.(Don't see the muffler of the madam is getting wrapped around the chain of your rikshaw- had you drawn the rikshaw for even a little moment, the other end of the muffler would have so tightly around her neck that she would have suffocated to die)' Harish said."Haan,haan, babu ji,(yes..yes I see.)" he said removing the dupatta from the jaw of the chain. Meanwhile, as he laid eyes on the most beautiful creation of almighty, a fair, probably a college girl, Harish couldn't help but be mesmerized by her beauty, her aura of confidence and grace. For a while Harish dreamt that the maiden beauty was walking across the S.S.L.N.T.College campus, her long, flowing hair dancing in the wind, her laughter ringing through the air. But beneath his infatuation, Harish carried a heavy burden. The memories of his traumatic past haunted him, leaving him feeling isolated and alone. He couldn't bear to confide in anyone, couldn't bring himself to share his pain and shame.

Suddenly, a sweet-pleasant voice vibrated his eardrum, "It took, me time to understand, what was happening? ...but, now clear to me, thank you so much for saving me, by the way, I am Sudha" As the voice compelled Harish to bring out of the dream, the fragrance of lavender faded away. Neither his answer," I am Harish." could now be audible to Sudha nor her magnetic and enthralling look could be visible to Harish. The vision of the posterior of the rikshaw had also disappeared in the college lane. Golden bells rang for many days in the minds of Harish but, day by day the sound of bells was compressed by some unknown burden he was carrying in his mind. In January, there was an annual function at the Patliputra Medical College, Dhanbad, Alka Yagnik and other famous Bollywood singers were invited to perform as well as judge the competition to be held. The main attraction of the function was the Inter College Singing Competition. All colleges of the locality were invited. Harish along with his elder brother entered the auditorium on the night of the singing competition event as he was a fan *of rising Bollywood singer Alka Ygyanik so specially he had gone to his brother for the event. Allotting a seat for Harish in the front row, his brother went out for his duties as a member of the host institute. After listening to three contestants, the anchor of the programme gave a thrilling announcement, " Now, ladies and gentlemen...after .. the melodious song sung by Ritu Mahato from R.S.P.College...please put your hands together for Sudha Mallick from S.S.LN.T College, she will sing Tu .. Ne ..Wo. Rangeeley ...from the film 'Kudarat'. As she started, whistles, clappings and loud appreciations echoed through the auditorium. Her beauty, her voice and her delicacy during the act fascinated Harish, he was completely spellbound and speechless. Alka Yagnik and other experts too appreciated Sudha's grace of singing on the stage. A feeling whether it was love or infatuation, Harish didn't know, flooded the young and innocent heart with gentle touches of tender sweet emotions. As soon as Sudha went backstage, his heart became void and wished he could meet her once. He stood to move away as now he couldn't involve himself in the programme as a good audience. While going through the aisle security gave a slip and said," Abhi, jo madam gaa rahi thee, oos madam ne bhijwaya hai." It was a pleasant surprise to Harish, now it was an Eureka moment to him, perhaps even Archimedes would not have been as happy with his discovery as Harish was at this moment. He came out and stood under the light post to read the note, it read,"* **Harish, I want to meet you, at Railway station platform number 4, near Sharma Book Stall, tomorrow at 9:00 A.M. And I am sorry, I secretly listened to you talking to Sarvesh Bhaiya near the backstage and hence knew your name. -SUDHA-"**

"What a meeting location !" uttered Harish with a naughty smile.

At that moment he dreamt, as Sudha reached out both her hands, he felt something stir within him. A glimmer of hope, a light in the darkness. And as Sudha wrapped her arms around him, offering him solace and understanding, Harish knew that he had found a guardian angel amid his despair.

On the other hand, he thought, "Meeting for what? Simply to thank me.", "no-no-no ..to thank only..why to meet?" "a note on the slip was enough". Ultimately he left everything in the hands of time and destiny.

The night was too long for both the love birds, Harish woke up very early - became ready- left the college hostel a -reached Dhanbad station at exactly 8:00 A.M., bought a platform ticket and finally reached the destination, Sharma Book Stall, at platform number 4. His heart was beating rapidly, so many pleasant and unpleasant thoughts were entering his mind and he evacuated it. His mother always gave him advice," Whenever you feel that you are getting blocked by thought -recite Hanuman Chalisa, slowly- there will be clarity." As soon as he remembered his mother's advice, he began with ..Jai Hanuman gyan gun-sagar, jai kapis ti hoon lok ujagar.. in his mind. On second thought his conscious mind doubted.."Will Brahmachari Baba Hanuman ji help him in this matter?".. Anyway, he suppressed his thought and sitting on the bench near the stall he continued to murmur Hanuman Chalisa.. once-twice-thrice went on. The announcement of the arrival of the Satabdi Express made him aware that it was about 9:30 AM as he knew that the scheduled arrival time of Shatabdi Express was 9:20 AM. He was to roll his eyes to watch time on the clock hanging on platform number 4, he found his diva standing near him, she was out of breath and unable to speak out. Finally spelt, "Sorry..sorry Harish...you know, coming out of the girls' hostel during the morning is so tough... I went through many ordeals to reach here, so I became delayed, I kept you waiting."

"Don't worry - you please, try to relax.. as I am quite okay." Harish consoled her. They walked toward the lonely godown in the platform area to avoid the crowd near the stall. They sat on the lonely lonely bench near the godown. Now Sudha had become comfortable. They shared their introductions -family backgrounds and many things. Sudha talked flawlessly during the meeting but Harish conversed less and kept himself a good listener of her beautiful accent and silent observer of her alluring beauty, thinking very highly about his fortune. The most painful part of their conversation was that Sudha had lost her mother in her childhood. She had been grown up by her stepmother. An unbelievable piece of information Sudha shared was that her mother had come in her dream after our first -accidental meeting, she hinted to her about our destiny. She said that she had found a true friend with whom she could share her pain. Wasn't it surprising?

Their love story had a tumultuous beginning, filled with pain but the innocence of adolescence through it all, Sudha stood by Harish's side, helping him heal and find the strength to move forward. And as their love blossomed and grew, they both knew they had found the missing pieces of their broken hearts in each other. Was it a true love or an infatuation at the dawn of manhood ?.. Time will tell us.

I thought in my mind that the play of Harish's was dramatized near my locality, the students' lodge where I stayed was in Heerapur, very close to S.S.L.N.T. College. As an excellent listener, I found myself deeply engrossed in the tale, pondering the intricacies of Harish's life. It was my misfortune that I remained oblivious to the subtle nuances of their love story.

The drum beat reminded us that it was time to attend the evening puja and aarti.

Both of us moved towards pandal where Harish was already there.

VIII

JANNIE'S TRANSGENDER CONNECTION

Now I want to draw your kind attention's to the things that are happening at present. All the staff members in my firm are quite efficient but I always appreciate Jannie the most, for her intelligence, hard work and dedication. She never leaves any stone unturned to get better results in any case. The Komal rape case was a piece of national news in 2020, the victim was from a village, close to my native place near Bokaro. On the way to home from her work, she took a bus, which had only four members in it, including the driver and conductor of the bus . All of them had brutally raped her one by one for four hours in the plying bus and she was thrown nude into the Damodar River, near Bijulia. She did not survive. In the days following the attack, newspaper reports elaborated on the gruesome nature of the rape. I can proudly say that our firm has won the case and attempted to give justice to the victim's family, only due to Jannie's sincere efforts, which I have credited, many times in local news channels for giving justice to the victim's family. As the case was high profile, the bus owner had deep political connections, we had to cross many ordeals and ultimately I turned out to be a well-known figure due to this case . My non-acceptance of any fees in such cases became national news. I had to clarify with media persons that my sources of income was from the revenue earned by companies to which the S.R. Associates provide legal advice. Gourang Mazumdar and Jannie had joined the firm on the same day, and Gourang had blamed me in an indirect way , at an office party, having given my special favour to Jannie and neglecting his efforts. But this was untrue. I favoured her for her dedication towards her job. There was another reason too, for favouring her unofficially, it is personal to my family.

At the beginning of my career, I was living with my wife and newly born son Pranav, in a small rented house in Nagratoli. Peter DeSouza and Maria DeSouza were a couple and our next-door neighbours. Sushma had developed a family relationship with the couple. Our son Pranav was only six months old. One day we were coming back after watching the movie Laalbadsah at Sujata Talkies. I was waiting in the traffic to disperse to drive my car ahead, suddenly I heard an infant crying near to me. I moved my eyes all around but nothing could be seen except a dustbin. The road was not clear from traffic so I could not drive any further. It was a sort of signal light near Lalpur Chawk and hinjras usually ask for money from taxis, auto-rikshaws etc. Suddenly my attention was attracted towards the dustbin, and what I saw ,was quite enough to condemn such an act performed by a human. A hijra was drawing a newborn baby from the dustbin and cleaning her, pampering her,.. directly came to me, I could not understand why it chose me as many vehicles were waiting to move ahead. The saviour God for the baby said to me," Babu ji, ye bachchi mar jayegi, rotey -rotey senseless ho gayi hai, ek- do din ki bachchi hai, ise rakh lo, babuji, ise bacha lo." I thought, 'Why, me?' and turned towards Sushma's eyes, tears were rolling down. Pranav was already sleeping on her lap. Meanwhile, traffic dispersed and vehicles started to move forward. Sushma saw the saviour running along the car which was just to move. 'Ise bacha lo ,bahen ji, ye mar jayegi babuji' . Due to the pathetic voice of the saviour Sushma could not resist herself and extended her arms outwards the car window and held the baby. We had come out of the traffic and then the car was in its pace. Inside the car we were speechless and the baby was senseless. I was controlling the steering, clutch, gear and brake only with the help of my subconscious mind. In between I sometimes observed Sushma's face and sometimes baby's face and adjusted the front mirror to Pranav sleeping at the back seat .Sushma was silent but my subconscious mind knew where to go first, of course, the hospital.

As Sushma held the newborn baby in his arms I couldn't help but feel a sense of fear and uncertainty creeping into his mind. The baby was uncovered, quite dirty, filled with dust rotten smell, but her aura was clear enough to be attractive to her. Slow-pitched lub tub sound from her heart was the only ray of hope for her in our minds. I was thinking of the cruelty of the mother who had put her in the dustbin, I questioned to myself, "Whatever the situation might be, how a human can be so self-centred?"The image of the transgender who had handed over the baby to Sushma, flashed before my eyes, and I couldn't shake off the thought that they were somehow involved in a sinister plot to steal children and raise them as beggars.

But as I looked down at the innocent face of the baby and realized that my assumptions were based on nothing but stereotypes and prejudice. The transgender who had given us the baby, had shown nothing but kindness and compassion, despite facing discrimination and hardship in their own life. I had a notion that they were not good humans, they stole children from the house to join them in their community for begging.

I began to question his beliefs and biases towards transgenders and realized that they were just like any other human being, capable of love, kindness, and empathy. The act of handing over the baby, despite their struggles, spoke volumes about the true nature of the transgender community.

Through this experience, my opinion towards transgenders underwent a complete transformation. I learned to see them not as outcasts or criminals, but as individuals who deserved respect and acceptance just like anyone else.

Finally, I realized that it was my ignorance and preconceived notions that had clouded my judgment. I vowed to challenge those beliefs and stand up for the rights and dignity of the transgender community, knowing that they were just as worthy of love and compassion as anyone else.

My subconscious mind led me to drive through Mahatma Gandhi Road road and ultimately stopped near the gate of Sadar Hospital. We both rushed toward the emergency ward leaving Pranav in the car. Doctor Sharma checked the baby properly and consoled us," Nothing to worry about." He called the nurse and told them something and went away. The nurse held both the legs of the baby, made upside down and kept it hanging for one minute the baby cried suddenly. The baby was then laid down, the nurse gave an injection, and finally, she advised about its immediate feeding. We came out near the car, Sushma was worrying about Pranav but he was safe in the car and still sleeping.

We came to our residence. Sushma first cleaned the baby's body with warm water and fed her milk with a spoon. Pranav had eaten nothing since evening but we kept sleeping as we had no energy to wake him up and serve food for him. Both Pranav and the baby were sleeping but Sushma and I were in deep thought of the new responsibility.

Sushma said, " Baby ko hum hi legally adopt kar lein? (Willn't it be better to adopt the baby legally?)" ..I was silent to the proposal of Sushma but no alternate could be sensed at that moment. After a while, I replied," Mujhe thoda sochne do... (Let me think for some time...)" I could not understand what was the will of God. The whole night we were in thinking mode. I better know what Sushma was thinking. We wished to have a boy and a girl child to complete our family as a happy family. After one year of our marriage, there was a miscarriage of her pregnancy there were lots of complications during Pranav's birth Doctors had warned us that the next pregnancy might be fatal to her. Adopting the baby was the best option for us to complete our family. But I could not overburden Sushma to look after two offerings, as she was not in a good phase of her health. A sudden thought about the DeSouza family came in my mind doctors have declared that Mrs DeSouza can't be a mother. They were thinking of IVF treatment. Finding Sushma, tossing on the bed and yet out of sleep,

I hinted the matter to her. I knew it was difficult for her. I could read that she dreamt something about the baby during these hours. I tried to convince her the whole night. Willingly or unwillingly she met her friend Maria early in the morning. Sushma's story and proposal were like a dream come true for DeSouzas. As I came from my routine daily walk I was surprised to see the baby smiling on the lap of Mrs DeSouza. She had already started to call the baby with the name Jannie.

This is how I have a personal relationship with Jannie. For Sushma, she is no less than her daughter. Pranav never felt the absence of a sister in his life. When Jannie comes to our bungalow at Namkum, we both wife and husband enjoy the squabbling, of an advocate and a police inspector, very much. Pranav is presently deputed at Simdega police station.

IX

COLLEGE LIFE NOSTALGIA

Namkum, a locality in Ranchi, is known for the innocence of its people. With a population of around 200,000, this area is renowned for its natural beauty. However, back in the 1990s, when we thought of buying a plot here, it was rather deserted. Sushma found this location suitable as per Vaastu norms, and thus, her dream home was built here. Since we were living in a rented house, Sushma used to plan daily how our home would look and how it would be decorated, and now, all her dreams materialized in this house bringing us endless peace.

Our friend and former neighbour, Mr De Souza, who is also Jannie's father and a civil engineer, contributed significantly to the design of our home, and the contribution of Amar Singh son of Mr Munna Singh,, the contractor and builder, cannot be forgotten. Our house serves as both our home and our office. In this house-cum-office, S R Associates has continued to grow and prosper by leaps and bounds. And how could it not, when our housewarming took place on June 21? June 21 is a special day in terms of geography(it is summer solstice), and the most unique thing is that it's also Harish's birthday. Sushma had selected this day as Harish had an unforgettable role in our lives, he was the one who recognised my law potential and brought my career on the right track as before my career was running on the confused track.

As the years passed, Namkum saw a surge in population, transforming the once quiet area into a bustling neighbourhood. Our house now is a sanctuary amidst the chaos of daily life. However, the peaceful ambience was recently disrupted by the loud sounds emanating from Vishnu Sounds, a nearby dance and music institute. The old Bollywood movies blared from the institute's speakers, often distracting Sushma.

As the echoes of Vishnu Sounds drifted through the air, they created distractions for my office staff members in their work. Gourang Mazumdar, a member of our legal team, sent complaints about the issue to the concerned authority in Ranchi Municipal Corporation.

Today, the loud voice of a song playing there was getting deep into my mind, and the rhythms of my heartbeat accompanied my mind as it walked me through memory lane. The song was "Tune O Rangiley Kya Jaadu Kiya....."

There was a miraculous connection between this song and the life of Harish.

My Memory Lane:

It was the 21st of June, and Virender, Harish, and I were sitting in the rented room at Lalpur. During their post-graduation, Virendra and Harish had rented this room. All three of us had just completed our post-graduation, and our results were about to be published. I had come to see them to learn about their future aspirations after post-graduation. Although we studied at the same university, my PG college was different from theirs; mine was in Dhanbad. Virendra and I had planned a surprise birthday celebration for Harish. Suddenly, the sound of the program "Binaca Geet Mala" being played on the radio in the neighbouring room drew our attention. It was the voice of Ameen Sayani: "Behno aur bhaiyo, toh... sunte hain 'Kudrat' film ka ye gaana, jise farmaish kiya hai... Jhumri Tilleya se... Bunty, Babloo, Pintoo aur saathiyon ne." The song started, "Tune wo rangile... kaisa jaadu kiya..."

It was a surprise to us; it was Harish's birthday, and his love story had a deep connection with the song. But the situation here was quite different; the nature of astonishment among the three of us was quite different. I was completely ignorant about the recent happenings in their lives. "The song on the radio was Sudha's way of celebrating Harish's birthday; now it's our turn to celebrate it," said Virender when Harish was not in the room. I was unable to understand what Sudha's contribution to this song was, which was played on the radio that day. Meanwhile, Harish had to go out to Cathedral to meet the Father Cristopher , so he left us for almost two hours. Now we had two hours to arrange the surprise birthday celebration. I noticed that both Harish and Virender were somehow upset, which made me uncomfortable too. Out of curiosity, I asked him, "Is anything wrong here?"

This question made Virendra burst into tears. His throat and lips almost refused to cooperate with his voice. As I made him comfortable, he said, "We've both lost hope in life; two events in our lives have completely ruined us,..one is connected to my life, and the other to the heart of Harish." He continued and asked which story I would prefer to hear first. Before I could give my preference, he started with his own but gave a statutory warning to make me strong enough to listen.

Story of own misfortune told by Virendra:

I had dreamt that after completing an M.Sc. in Mathematics, I would become a lecturer in some college and support my father financially, as you know they are deep in debt. But fate had something else in store.

That day was the fourth day of our final exam. The examination room was silent, and there was anxiety on everyone's faces. The question paper was very difficult, and as usual, everyone had brought cheats with them. The look on everyone's faces showed that the answers to the questions asked weren't in their cheating materials.

Suddenly, I remembered that the answer to Question 4 of the paper was in my right sock. I took it out, placed it under my answer sheet, and started writing quickly. In this process, I didn't realize that a flying squad team from the university head office had arrived. One of the team members saw me cheating through the window from the corridor. He suddenly entered the room and snatched my answer sheet away from me.

I suddenly became angry as usual due to my ill temper and, while trying to snatch my sheet back, threatened him and used abusive language for him, which was my biggest mistake. He took my sheet, stapled the cheat sheet to it, and announced that I was expelled from the exam and would not be allowed to take any exams from any university for the next three years. If I hadn't gotten angry and had requested him instead, the situation might have been under control. Now, three or four team members took me to the principal like a criminal. I requested them a lot, but they spoke to the principal, prepared some paperwork, and sealed my expulsion. Perhaps the principal had no choice either, and I was finally expelled for three years.

This news was spread throughout the whole college like firewood. Now I could not apply for a job even through my graduation degree in the locality. In this way, I got ruined forever.

I was really sad for Virendra, I said," What next?"

Virendra said," I don't know. I have left everything on Harish."

He composed himself, then said, "Let's start preparing for the surprise birthday celebration."

For this very purpose, Virendra had specially written a letter to call me, because he knew that my presence on his birthday would help Harish feel a bit lighter in that sorrowful atmosphere.

The two of us prepared everything together, and as soon as he arrived, we gave him a surprise. He liked our gift, especially this gesture from us. Suddenly, the atmosphere felt a bit festive. That night, Harish and I slept in the same room, while Virendra was in the next room. I couldn't sleep; two things were making me restless. First, Harish had never used to go to church before, but now he has suddenly started visiting and talking with the Father, which surprised me. The second thing was what happened: Harish's life was falling apart.

I finally asked, "Why did you go to church?... Why is your interest in Christianity growing? ?"

He replied, "I enjoy talking to Father Christopher... he has a doctorate degree in the Ramayana... ais aura is so clear and bright that meeting him brings great peace... there's so much to learn from him."

Once my first question was answered, I quickly asked him another, "How's Sudha doing? ..When are you thinking about marriage?" My question seemed to unsettle him, but he replied with a pained smile, "Forget about me; tell me about Tripurna—how is she?" I sensed he was avoiding my question. I smiled and said, "Come on, that was just childhood, a childhood crush... it feels nice to think about the same for a few days, maybe even years, but as soon as you come to your senses, you just laugh at yourself."

Neither of us could sleep, so I finally asked the question that had been on my mind for hours, "When I came here, I saw a nameplate carrying the name-'Munna Singh' on the gate of the next door building .. is this the same Munna Singh whose name frequently appears in the local newspapers for hooliganism and dirty politics?"

His answer was, "You guessed it right."

He continued," If you can't sleep, would you like to hear a love story?" My interest was piqued, and I agreed.

A love story told by Harish:

Hero-Virendra Saxena

Heroin-Suhani Singh

Villain-Present: Harish Raajdan

Future: The Munna Singh

The previous winter was going on, and every afternoon, Virendra used to go up to the terrace under the pretence of studying for exams in the warmth of the sun. I was quite pleased, thinking he was serious about his preparation. One day, while he was studying on the terrace, I also felt like joining him in the sun to study, as I was having a feeling of cold inside the room. When I went up, I was surprised to find that something else was being studied there—this was the study of love.

There was a beautiful girl on Munna Singh's terrace, and Virendra was busy admiring her. And, as I sensed, it seemed that the girl also enjoyed being admired by him.

When I asked Virendra about it, he brushed it off. I knew it was wrong because he was already married, regardless of the circumstances of his marriage. He shouldn't have been cheating on his wife, Anita, at any cost. But things didn't stop there; they continued gazing at each other secretly. After a month of this hide-and-seek, one day Virendra tossed a note folded in a piece of paper. At first, the girl acted indifferent, but she discreetly picked up the note. The next day, another note arrived but it was from Munna Singh's terrace—a love letter revealing her name, the name that had annoyed my ears countless times. That name was Suhani. I tried to scare him by talking about Munna Singh, reminding him of Anita Bhabhi's life, but nothing seemed to work. Then, suddenly, something happened in his life that I'll tell you about some other time, and it gave me an idea to save his married life. Now, we're planning to leave Ranchi and go to Delhi to prepare for competitive exams. Once he gets a job, everything will be fine. Leaving the city will get Suhani off his mind. Lately, at least, I haven't had to listen to his endless rants about love and big romantic speeches.

After the story, Harish said, "I'd say, you should come with us to Delhi too; let's crack some exams together."

I said," I will talk to my father about it."

After the story, Harish had fallen asleep, but there was no sleep in my eyes. My mind was restless, constantly turning over the events happening here. I was especially troubled, wondering what could have happened in Harish's life that Virendra was hinting at.

I had slept late at night, so I woke up late in the morning. What did I see? In the veranda, there were 30-40 plastic chairs set up, and one slightly nicer chair with cushions on it. Some people were sitting on the plastic chairs; there was a Sikh gentleman who seemed to be there with his family. I was a bit surprised, thinking, "What's going on here?" People were arriving slowly, and the chairs were filling up. I was puzzled, so I asked Virendra, "What's happening here today?"

Virendra said," Today, it is Sunday and every Sunday Harish will have to give the sermon."

"Sermon,.. what type of sermon?" And you landlord permit all these things?" I was surprised.

"Let a day pass; slowly, you'll understand everything." Virendra tried to quench my thirst for query.

Along with the people I took a chair and sat.

Sermon by Harish:

I am grateful to all of you for gathering here to listen to someone as ordinary as me. I am much younger than many of you, yet it's your greatness that you trust me. I am neither a saint nor a wise person; I simply come before you with pure intention. I am especially thankful to Sardar Jaskeerat Ji, though I don't know why he places so much faith in me. Our topic for today is, 'What is Truth?'"

Truth is often viewed as something absolute, unwavering, and universal. But the journey to understand and live by truth is deeply personal. For some, truth lies in the pursuit of knowledge, and for others, it rests in the values and principles they hold dear. Truth, in essence, is not just about accuracy but about authenticity—it is the harmony between what we believe, what we say, and what we do.

In a world where opinions and facts are often mixed, distinguishing truth from illusion becomes challenging.

To illustrate the concept of truth, I present a story to you.

All of you must have heard of King Harishchandra .....

The sermon was going on and I enjoyed it at the same time amazed of this version of Harish but Virendra, inside the room, called me with facial expressions to come inside for tea as I had not taken even morning tea.

Offering tea, Virendra could sense that I was troubled by my curiosity about Harish's transformation. He said, "Have some tea; there's no need to go outside. I will quench all your curiosities." I just looked at him—a lover boy, a mere puppet in the hands of fate. He said he would tell me everything, but I was advised to strengthen my heart.

I have read R.K. Narayan's book' Guide' and also watched the movie of the same name, which features Dev Anand. Raju's character came to my mind, though here, Harish was different from Raju from the very beginning. However, in both situations, due to a change of heart, both eventually become spiritual guides.

Story of the birth of a Divyatma told by Virendra:

The love between Sudha and Harish was innocent, but who knew that nature was conspiring against them? A photograph resembling Sudha in the "missing persons" column of a Hindi newspaper—reporting the disappearance of a girl from the SSLNT College hostel—shook his life to its core. He immediately took the first available bus to Dhanbad but made me swear not to come along, saying, "One should resolve the fundamental issues of life on their own." How could we ever challenge his principles? He returned after about 10 days, and his shared story shook me.

He said that he tried to meet Sudha's room partner, Jasmine, as soon as he reached the college but security norms there, due to this case, had been made strict that no outsider, other than the parents of candidates, could meet any hotelier. But Jasmine managed to give a letter to Harish, through a peon, describing everything.

In the letter, he explained that Sudha had been followed by several men for days. They would make vulgar comments, and one day, they taunted her by saying that she was wasting her time with Harish, calling him a simpleton. They mocked her, saying she should be with someone "smart" like them, who she didn't even look at. One of the stalkers even went as far as to say that they always get what they want, one way or another, and they said that people tremble in front of the master. After that, she stopped coming to her hostel room for several days. The BA final exams were going on, and it was only when she was absent for the Political Science paper that everyone realized she was missing.

A few days later, the same newspaper reported, "The body of the girl missing from SSLNT College hostel was found in Bekar Bandh." This news nearly drove him mad. He went to Dhanbad alone once again in the tense atmosphere of the cities and returned after three days, but he never told anyone what had happened there. For the next three days, he locked himself in his room without food or water.

You already know that on October 31, when our then-Prime Minister, Mrs. Indira Gandhi, was brutally assassinated by her Sikh bodyguards, tensions rose across all cities. Looting incidents were happening against Sikh families, their homes were being attacked, and people were breaking in to harass their daughters and women. It was the night of November 3, around midnight, when, somehow, Harish brought a Sikh family to our home. The family included a husband, wife, and their two young daughter

After locking them in his room, he knocked on my door. As I woke up, I was already scared by the noise outside, but the moment I opened the door, Harish told me everything—how he had rescued the family from the mob and brought them to his home. I felt relieved, not only because he had saved them, but also because, after days of silence, Harish had finally started speaking again.

I was anxious, wondering what would happen in the morning. Our landlord would surely evict us, and our *neighbours wouldn't spare us either for sheltering a Sikh family. We kept watch all night to ensure no one from outside would discover we were hiding them. But when our landlord found out in the morning, and we had to face him, I was astonished to see a different side of Harish—a person who spoke so little in life was able to convince him with such resolve. As a result, our landlord joined us in our mission, and together, we all kept the family hidden. Their food used to come from the landlord's house, and eventually, once the situation calmed down, the family was safely sent back to their home.*

From that day onward, the head of the Sikh family, named Sardar Jaskirat Singh, started referring to Harish as "Divyatma" (a divine soul). He began arranging for Harish to give discourses everywhere and organized religious gatherings in his honour. Now, even though Harish doesn't want it, he behaves like a saint.

When I was listening to Harish's story of losing his love, I felt regret that I was right there where so many events took place, yet I remained completely unaware. Harish neither asked for help nor did I come to know anything.

Virendra said," You can see Sardarji outside in the audience, he is Jaskirat Singh, him I was talking, he is one the greatest fan of Harish, he can go to any extent to help him."

Out of curiosity, I said, " Does Harish not intend to convert this into his profession?"

"Nah, he thinks of coming out of this labyrinth," Virendra replied.

The sermon from outside was still echoing in my ears; he was explaining to the audience how life becomes easier when one speaks the truth.

But Virendra told me something that shook me to the brain completely. He said, "Sudha appears in his dreams every night, and as he sleeps, they talk as if they are two living people having a conversation. I've told everyone in the house about it, they have felt and witnessed them talking and they were all astonished... You already know that he always had recurring dreams of a train... Now, a new dream has become a part of his life every night. The people you see outside will soon be joined by others, who will come with their problems. They'll write down their issues on slips and give them to Harish. In his dream, Harish will discuss them with Sudha, and by next Sunday, they'll each receive solutions to their problems."

I was astonished and was just about to bid farewell to Lalpur (which is presently only a few kilometres from my house) for two days filled with surprising happenings and experiences, when the sound of my favourite song from Vishnu Sounds, "Jaago Mohan Pyaare..." pulled me out of my college memories. Sung by Lata Mangeshkar, it's a song of Raj Kapoor's film is very near to my heart, but due to some issue with the instruments, the sound was coming out somewhat harsh, easily snapping me out of my dream world. Yet, in those half-hour memories, I had lived through years of life.

X

A VISIT TO THE NATIVE PLACE

My ancestral house is at Ranipokhar village near Bokaro, during my childhood days it was a small village with kaccha houses but today it is the village for the name only , its boundaries almost touch Bokaro city and the transformation part is that no kaccha houses can be seen in the village, big buildings, overhead water tanks, roofs with dish antennas, 24x7 electric supply and good wi-fi connectivity have made the village extraordinary from an ordinary village. I was born and brought up there. Whenever I miss the sweet earthy fragrance of the soil I visit here. After the death of the parents, the visits are not so frequent. This was the special occasion of a marriage in the family so everyone had gathered. I usually set out on a drive with Pranav, whenever I visit here. Today Pranav was driving and I was describing how they have changed since my childhood. I said," Bokaro- today is better known as Bokaro Steel City. earlier known by the name Marafari, which was a small settlement in the then Dhanbad district. After the independence of India, Pt. Nehru planned to set up in India and Bokaro Steel Ltd. was built in 1964 which was later acquired by Steel Authority of India." I was giving such pieces of information about the place during the drive, which Pranav already knew or didn't know, I had no idea but he behaved like a good listener. We reached our usual destination i.e. City Park. Pranav parked the car and we were just to enter the park gate A boy, dark in colour, tall and thin physique, rushed to me and touched my feet. I could not recognise him, still said," Who are you? How can I help you?" His humble answer was," Sir, who doesn't know you? You are no less than God to my family. I am Prakash, Komal's brother." I asked with surprise," Which Komal?" " Sir, you are the one who fought for justice for my victimised and dead sister," he explained further. I suddenly collected my memory and understood that he was rape victim Komal's brother. Finding no interest in our ongoing talks Pranav, started moving here and there near the colourful rose plants in the park. Pranav has developed an excellent appreciation and liking for varieties of roses, perhaps he has inherited this quality from Sushma, I must say he is the rare and unique combination of a police inspector and a rose lover.

My conversation continued, with Prakash and finally, I came to know that he was working in Bangalore as a delivery boy. I recalled Jannie's description of her Bangalore visit during Nitin's Divorce case and finally connected all the dots. I came to know that Prakash had left Bengaluru city to look after his parents. His father had been blind and Komal was the only earning member of the family. After getting the compensation from her case the eyes of the father were operated on, which was the aim of Komal's life and he has got partial vision now. But the family is still suffering in poverty. The State Government had formed Komal Charitable Trust to help such victims but all these things are still in the file of government. The family had lost its daughter and its earnings. Prakash was deprived of his right to education and turned into a livelihood earner for the family at such an early age. Presently he had no job and from his talks I came to know that he badly needed a job for survival and supporting his family. I suddenly collected my memor ,who could help him, and of a sudden, I thought of Virendra, although our friendship had stood in formal mode still I knew he could help, after all, he is not less than the owner of a private steel plant near Bokaro, and he must manage a job for Prakash in his plant or office. I gave him my mobile number and told me to make a call to me and in this way, we shared each other our numbers. I assured him to search for a job for him. I departed him with a heavy heart for the young boy.

As I remembered his nickname,' Byomkesh Bakshi,' as Jannie had told me, I started to think of his requirement for my firm too. Still, the thought of his joining Virender's company was more appealing to me than joining my firm as for joining my firm, he has to leave his native place and shift to Ranchi. I was a little bit selfish that he might collect the shreds of evidence in Nitin's case after a few months if needed.

As I approached Pranav in the serene rose garden, I was met with a heartwarming sight. There he was, cradling an injured squirrel in his gentle hands, tending to its wounds caused by the thorns of the roses. The compassion and kindness in his actions stirred a deep emotion within me. At that moment, I realized that Pranav, like a coconut, displayed a tough exterior but harboured a heart of gold within.

I stood in awe, watching as he patiently cared for the little creature until it was ready to be set free. It was a testament to his character as a police inspector, showcasing a rare and admirable quality of empathy towards all beings. Not wanting to interrupt this tender moment, I silently observed until the squirrel was safely released back into the garden.

With a soft smile, I shared a tidbit of folklore with Pranav, informing him of the special blessings that squirrels are said to possess from Lord Rama. To my surprise, he was already aware of the story from a spiritual gathering of our 'Guruji' he had attended. His understanding of the squirrel's significance in assisting in the construction of the bridge to Lanka resonated deeply with me.

I reflected on the lesson learned from this encounter - the importance of showing gratitude for even the smallest acts of kindness or support, without expecting anything in return. Pranav nodded in agreement, embodying the spirit of gratitude and compassion in his actions. In that fleeting moment, amidst the beauty of the rose garden, I felt a profound connection with both Pranav and the squirrel, grateful for the reminder of the power of kindness and appreciation in the world.

We were running behind schedule, caught up in the many rituals that required our presence at home. It was my niece Amrita's wedding, just one year younger than her cousin Pranav. Participating in family functions like these helps strengthen the bonds between us. I could feel an emotional attachment of Amrita with Pranav.

The week-long festivities came to an end with Amrita's tearful farewell, a poignant moment as she was the cherished daughter of the family for so many years. As we set off for Ranchi the day after the wedding, we left behind the familiar scent of our homeland, holding onto the memories in our hearts.

I was carrying one more thought with me from my native land, and think Sushma too was carrying the same thought, during the Haldi ceremony of Amrita ,everyone was asking from Pranav when would he marry. Pranav , with no answer, kept smiling at everyone's question, but I and maybe Sushma's minds got preoccupied with the topic of his marriage. Everyone has been discussing who the girl will be for the marriage, but I don't know and not yet ever thought of it . I also don't know when the marriage will happen, but one thing I do know is what kind of girl should be chosen. She should be beautiful, cultured, educated, willing to follow old traditions while also adapting to the new times, religious, loving towards flowers and compassionate towards all living beings. This is what Pranav likes. I don't know when we will find this perfect combination, or maybe Pranav has already chosen someone and told his mother, but not me. No, no, if that were the case, Sushma would have definitely told me. These thoughts played mischief in my mind all the way.

XI

JOB OF OFFICE ASSISTANT

I was to take a return drive from Bokaro after attending a meeting with the client I had to go back to Ranchi as this time I was going to avoid the visit to Ranipokhar. I, from time to time encountered the thought of the job search for Prakash, whose innocence had a special print on my heart. On the way it fell, the main office premises of Bokaro Steel Works Private Limited, Virendra's office. I was in confused mode, whether to meet him or not. All of a sudden, on the way, I saw Ajit, near the office parking who glanced at me first as my car was very slow in the office road. Ajit is a common school friend of Virendra and me. At the school hostel, everyone was jealous of my friendship with Harish and Ajit was their mastermind. I can not forget an event, for no reason, Ajit had slapped Harish

and he was warned to disconnect the friendship with me. But nobility and kindness with Harish let him forget everything very soon.

'Raaj..Raaj... ' Ajit's voice compelled me to apply the brake. He greeted me and shook hand with me with his left hand as I knew him he was not a lefty, as I moved toward his other hand I saw it was hanging through a splint belt, on the way to the office of Virendra I asked him," What happened to your right hand?".I was completely dazzled by the sparkle and glamour of his office, and his status, which made me dizzy. Meanwhile, Ajit responded to my question but the response was completely unnoticed by me. I had heard a lot about Virendra, and his fame, he had come to my office several times before, for Nitin's case, but I didn't realize how big a man he was. Now I feel like he suppressed all of us, I was feeling good for him.

Ajit headed me towards Virendra's office and on the way I came to know that he was an employee there. As soon as Virendra saw me, he also became very happy and excited and stood to hug me, with a warm welcome he said sarcastically, 'Where did the sunrise today that I suddenly got to see you? He took great care of me and left no shortcomings in taking care of me. In the meantime, Ajit said, 'Any news of your friend Harish?' Before I could say anything, Virendra said, 'No one will talk about him today, today after years, we have gathered together, let's talk about something else.' Ajit, let me tell you, I keep track of even my enemies, listen to me," He retired from LIC, he was a great speaker of the organisation and an amazing motivator for all India LIC staff members, he was given a two-year extension after retirement and he is still honoured as a chief guest most of the LIC events, ok ."

The inquiry about Harish's well-being from Ajit seemed too mechanical but Virendra's reaction toward him was original, The atmosphere started suffocating me, as it became intolerable to me to listen to any wrong word for

Harish, but his final gesture confused me whether Virendra hated him or appreciated him. I was trying to steer the conversation towards my point. I said, "Viru, there's a boy here, Prakash, who doesn't have much education... Oh, you must have heard about the Komal rape case, he is the victim's brother, he used to work as a delivery boy in Bangalore, he is quite intelligent." Before I could finish my sentence, he interrupted, "Raaj, you have come at the right time, I was just talking to Ajit about posting a job vacancy for an office assistant on social media."... He suddenly stopped talking and said, "He has an issue with his education... well, since you are here, let's do something about it... Send him to my office tomorrow, he can start working from tomorrow, but we will have to follow some company norms to make him permanent." The company will provide computer training from tomorrow and he has to go through open learning for formal education, the office will provide him with the necessary support, and don't worry, his salary package will not disappoint you." He said to Ajit," Go to Malti Kumbhakar's cabin, please and go through her files and check the inputs of the ongoing Coal Project, tomorrow is the last day of project submission, we can't take any risk in this project.' As he went out Virendra continued," I needed privacy so sent him out, ..Raaj, the hearing date for Nitin's case is approaching, and this time I want confirmation of his divorce." I said, "I am studying every aspect of the case, but I am confused, why should I prove asexuality, I just want a divorce?" He suddenly replied, 'Both are important to me, you might be a little confused...after the decision of the case, I will tell you my dilemma, just wait till the conclusion of the case.'

I left his office satisfied that Prakash would get a good job and that I could use him as a spy at the office to collect pieces of evidence for Nitin's case. This time, I again relied on Sushma's instinct that Nitin's case was somehow linked to Virendra's office. Ajit was on the way to see me off, I said to him," You have not told me what happened to your right hand .", he smiled and said," I told but you did not listen to me... Anyway...it is the outcome of my karma, it is the hand which I had used to slap an innocent fellow,...poor Harish," He continued, "We were on a trip to Uttrakhand mountains, at Pithoragarh our tourist bus was caught in a severe landslide, a huge rock collided to our bus but it reflected sideways sparsely hitting my window pan, everyone was at great panic, but for God sake every one was safe including my family members. My eyes were flickering for the close and safe look of my family members. " His story was quite adventurous as well as tragically panicable. Out of curiosity, I asked, "Then..?" He continued with the story as we both were standing in my car and I was opening its gate," I was so worried about my wife Antara, my son Rahul, and daughter Ruhi that I didn't even realize that my right hand got stuck badly between the window and the seat rod of the bus, the glass broke and many pieces of glass went inside. There was a lot of bleeding, I was taken to the hospital, and had surgery, for 6 months, in Delhi, Ranchi, and everywhere I underwent treatment, finally, doctors gave up and I got completely paralyzed. I feel I have received the fruits of my karma in this life in this way." I had mixed feelings of pain for Ajit and a sense of contentment for Harish I patted his back with the gesture of consolation and in this way, I got separated. I had already unlocked the car from a distance while deeper in the story of Ajit, I flung open the door, sat on the seat wrapped the seat belt and clamped it. Before I started the car, I remembered the story that Harish had told me, about the reason for not giving any reply, to the response of Ajit's slap on that very cool day.

One day Bhagawan Sri Krishna, while eating, suddenly left his food and started to leave somewhere. Mata Rukmini asked, "Swami, where are you going suddenly leaving your food?" He replied, "One of my devotees is in trouble, someone is attacking him." But he returned after reaching the door, upon which Mata Rukmini asked again, "Why did you come back, Swami?" Then Bhagwan answered," Now the devotee does not need my help, he has picked up a stone for his help."

Many times Harish used to tell me stories from our religious text during school days, I don't know from where he collected the stories then, but I understood the actual reference of the story told on that very day.

I started the car and l was pondering over the idea of whether using Prakash for a personal job pretext was appropriate, or if it could lead to betrayal with Virendra. But my heart was saying, this is the right thing to do, for collecting the real information for Nitin's case and Prakash's future too. Then I will be cautious to ensure that Prakash remains within the boundaries of trust and does not indulge himself in Byomkesh Bakshi-type spying.

The best part was that Prakash could look after his parents by doing his job in the local city.

I was in deep thought while driving back to Ranchi, how Virendra managed to establish such a big empire of wealth. People have many stories of acquiring the company Chhettals illegally but I knew he must have done something within the boundaries of the law. I remembered, which Harish used to say, " One day you will be the owner of such huge wealth that you will face problems in handling it." His statement proves true.

How can I suspect his divine words?

XII

DELHI COACHING CENTRE EPISODE

The news of the deaths of three IAS aspirants in Delhi saddened people across India. People from small towns send their children to Delhi for coaching after facing many difficulties and nurturing big dreams in their eyes. Today, all parents are going through a sense of insecurity. Watching the news on television repeatedly, Sushma was quite upset for the families who sent their children for coaching so they could lead a prestigious life ahead. We were sitting on the lawn in the evening with tea, and she became quite emotional and said, "You also struggled a lot in Delhi. You never told me much about life in Delhi in so many years. Today, tell me your whole story." Even after so many years of marriage, I had not told Sushma about it ... yes .. Harish and Virendra's stories are often told. Sushma comes from a very wealthy and affluent family, so I never wanted to make her sad with my hardships although she has faced ups and downs at the beginning of my career.

Our Delhi dilemma delivered by me to Sushma:

Virendra and Harish had already decided to go to Delhi for coaching classes after their post-graduation exams. I also presented the same proposal to my father, who readily accepted it. I accompanied my friends to Delhi as well. They had already managed to get a room at Mukherji Nagar for a very reasonable rent, with the help of connections from Sardar Jaskirat Singh of Ranchi, who was a great fan of Harish. His connections also helped Harish find some home tuition for survival. I used to get money for expenses from my father, while Virendra had no financial source. We managed everything from the resources of Harish and me. We all had our own challenges. Studying general knowledge, mathematical ability, etc., which were demanded by most competitive exams, was boring for me. Virendra sometimes felt saddened by the memory of his wife, Anita, and sometimes cursed his fate for not being able to have his beloved Suhani in his life. Those days we didn't have mobile phones that could have made life easier for Virendra, allowing him to regularly talk to Anita to avoid depression. He was derailing himself day by day, while I was trying to concentrate on my studies. We focused on qualifying for bank probationary exams. Harish was good at math but had to invest a significant amount of his time tutoring school students to meet almost half of our expenses. However, on our first attempt, we all failed to pass the exams.

Eventually, I was losing interest, but one day Harish brought the form and prospectus of LLB from the faculty of law at DU. He insisted I fill out the admission form, recognizing my extraordinary inclination and calibre for law and justice. After doing post-graduation, investing years in LLB, an internship under a lawyer, and a long process to establish myself, I was confused. He said, "It is never too late in life." I always believed he had a special blessing from God, and I never ignored his suggestions, as he had a good knowledge of Hindu scriptures. I remembered his statement from the mythological story of Sunita and Vinita, where Arun was born disabled due to Vinita's loss of patience. Finally, I filled out the form and got admitted to the law faculty at DU. Sushma, I can't tell you how my studies turned into fun at that time. It was then that I realized the importance of choosing a subject to study based on a real love for the subject. In those days, we often chose subjects or courses based on our parents' wishes or friends' choices. The purpose of education for most middle-class students was to secure a government job. I had gone to Delhi because my friends were going, and I wanted to obtain a well-paying government position.

After a year of dedication and hard work, Harish was selected as an assistant administrative officer in LIC. During his training period, he was posted at the Nizamuddin branch and consequently appointed to the same branch.

I was happy with my classes and studies. I started to get recognition in the class by the students ts and teachers too which was a new feeling for me and boosted me to work harder and harder.

Harish was also starting to feel the importance of financial security in life, as his parents, who completely neglected him, had also started talking to him. He was living in guilt and was now fueled by the desire to change his circumstances. His family had started looking for potential brides for him. He would use his salary to cover Virendra's expenses and send one-fourth of his salary back home. However, Virendra was beginning to feel neglected. He was becoming envious of both of us. He held Harish responsible for all his failures, when I listened to Virendra, I too started considering him guilty of his such conditions ,recalling his dreaful dream and thiking Harish as the lineman of the dream. Virendra even started blaming him for not being able to meet Suhani. He was quick to point out faults for minor things and I too became responsible for his failure, in his eyes. In truth, he was barely tolerating our happiness and his frustration. We all three had different boiling points which compelled us to react or boil differently in the same situation.

Virendra had always had high ambitions and was slowly getting victimised by it, he was losing patience. Assurances were made by Harish that if kept patience, he would have all the luxuries of life but always suggested waiting till destiny calls, but all were getting in vain.

One day, being out of control he said, "I don't trust destiny or its fake calls, you take a 3 lakh loan from LIC for me and I will do business with it, otherwise I will not spare you, I will ruin you."

It had become dawn on the lawn, the combination of lower air temperature, clear sky and higher relative humidity in the winter season was creating optimal conditions of dew formations which both of us felt together on our palms so we decided to go inside the house leaving my story half told.

XIII
THE NEW JOB

Prakash was very happy about getting a job in the native town. He was enjoying his job. With his pleasant behaviour, activeness and magnificent calibre he won the hearts of many in the office. His detective-like nature was helping a lot in the office. Soon, he became a favourite to the staff members and visitors in Virendra's office. Prakash always noticed that an old and dark-complexioned lawyer would often come to his office. As he had completed computer training, so he was deputed to Virendra's nearby cabin to assist his PA. The lawyer would often talk about legal matters, especially related to potential complications in wills. Prakash didn't understand these conversations. Once, when I called to get an update on his job, he told me a lot. Besides wills, the special topic that always came up in their discussions was the LGBTQA community. My head was spinning, as there seemed to be some connection between all these discussions and Nitin's divorce case. I couldn't understand why I was Virendra's choice for the case. He is such a big businessman, he could have easily found thousands of better lawyers than me, so why me?

As far as I know, the real owner of Virendra's steel company was Mr. Vishesh Chhattal. Virendra had won over Mr. Chhattal's heart so he entrusted the responsibility of overseeing this unit in Bokaro to Virendra. One more vital piece of information which I collected through my sources was that Mr Chhattal had no children and he had a long pending court case against his wife. After Mr Chhattal died in a road accident last year some news of the company's heir was published in local newspapers. But paid little attention.

I had clearly explained to Prakash that he should never take any step for me that goes against the company's principles and if his heart tells him that it is wrong. I needed information for Nitin's case, so I tried to think out of the box and sought help from Prakash. Shushma and I both believed that he could be the better source of collection pieces of information for the case. But Prakash and I had to keep in mind our respective limits.

Prakash is a little stubborn. He said on the phone, "Sir, you have done everything possible to bring justice to my sister. If I can help you in any way, my life will be blessed. Sir, please don't worry, the hardships of life have taught me the difference between right and wrong. Sir, I have my open education exam next month, the centre is in Ranchi, I am coming there and I hope to come with some important leads."

After a month, Prakash came. I had arranged for him to stay in my guestroom because the exams were going on for 15 days, staying in a hotel would be very expensive for him, besides he had taken a 15-day leave from the office, so his salary would also be deducted. This boy has become very near and dear to me in a very short time.

I gave special instructions to him," Remove everything regarding our case from your mind and focus only on your studies, during these examination days after that we will sit together to discuss case-related issues."

After his examinations were over, Prakash, Jannie and I assembled in the guest room at night and went through the pieces of evidence that he had collected during his months of job

Disclosure made by Prakash:

*I have been given the responsibility of handling the office files digitally and manually. During my office job, I came across many vital information which might be helpful to you. **First information:** Virendra Sir had been accused in Ranchi's Suhani abduction case years ago. In the 1980s, on a cold winter night, Virendra Sir was arrested from the Sisai Hotel in Ranchi as he was found in suspicious situations with a young and beautiful widow, Suhani Singh. However, he was granted bail when Suhani Madam stated in court, "I was with Virendra with my consent as I love him." Despite numerous charges filed by Munna Singh against Sir, he was ensnared in legal complications. The cases and trials continued for many years, and after Munna Singh's death, due to lack of evidence against Sir, the abduction case and other cases were temporarily closed by the court.*

Second information:

The real owner of Bokaro Steel Works Pvt Limited was Vishesh Chhettal, who died in a car accident without leaving any heirs to run his company. Mr. Chhattal had a close relationship with Virendra Sir, whom he considered like a son. Therefore, he entrusted all responsibilities of his company to him, although officially he was just the caretaker. Mr Chhattal had made a will just after his divorce from his wife, stating that after his death, the company would be managed by Mr

Virendra Saxena for two years. During this time, Mr. Saxena would not use any company funds for personal use. He would only be entitled to his salary as per company rules. Additionally, within the two years, Mr Saxena would be responsible for finding a capable and honest individual from the LGBTQA community to appoint as CEO of the company. The appointment would be subject to approval by the board members, who would assess the qualifications and integrity of the candidate.

The pieces of information given were quite important and my mind started connecting dots to get a lead for Nitin's case. Jennie said," Sir, we got the cause behind the Virenra sir's intention of proving Nitin an asexual is almost clear but we have just, information, not pieces of evidence,"

I responded, "Jannie, you are right, but we cannot compel Prakash to involve himself in more illegal activities." Prakash then explained, "I struggle with English, so I have difficulty understanding the key points in many documents that come my way." He then asked, "May I share some documents with you digitally, sir?"

I exclaimed, "No, no, absolutely not. You must be very cautious of your boundaries."

Lost in my thoughts and pondering over the unanswered questions from the conversation, I wondered about Suhani's fate, Virendra's resistance to her allure, Harish's failed attempts to keep him away from extramarital affairs, and what ultimately happened to Suhani.

Meanwhile, Jannie inquired, "Prakash, could you gather some information from Gopalan Florenza Apartment in Electronic City, Bengaluru?"

Prakash replied, "Of course, ma'am. I have been delivering food to many families there for three years and have built a good reputation."

Jannie then asked, "Have you met IT consultant Mr Nitin from room 304 of Gopalan FlorenzaApartment?"

Prakash expressed surprise, "Are you referring to Nitin Bhaiya? What a wonderful person he was! Unfortunately, his wife and newly born baby were abducted by a gangster, and shortly after I had to leave Bengaluru.

As he recalled the incident, Prakash speculated, "Ma'am, are we gathering evidence for Nitin bhaiya's divorce case? His wife, Ms. Somya, was abducted. But I heard we are looking for clues related to Nitin Bhaiya and Dr. Andy Kar …..I am a little bit confused" Turning to me, caught in my inner turmoil, he continued, "Sir, I am willing to go above and beyond any limit to gather information. I am thinking about the well-being of my boss's son."

I chuckled, "Never attempt to breach the boundaries."

While departing Prakash assured us that he would leave no stone unturned to collect the pieces of information from the office as well from the apartment at Bengaluru. He said," I have good connections there, maximum pieces of information can be collected through mobile phone,…and if needed I will go there."

Jannie, at the end, asked Prakash to find the present office address of Nitin and share it with her.

After two hours of departure from us Jannie got a WhatsApp message," Building No-4, Rajiv Gandhi Infotech Park, MIDC Phase 3, Main Road, Hingewadi-411057, Nitin bhaiya's address."

The second message followed: 'I will send his home address very soon.'

XIV

NEXT HEARING OF THE DIVORCE CASE

Prakash and Jannie were both very serious about Nitin's case. Prakash had also given Jannie, Nitin's home address through his sources. Nitin decided to go to Bangalore to investigate further. So, Jannie went to Pune and Prakash went to Bangalore.

Prakash, went to the Infosys office about which Jannie had told him. As soon as he enters the reception, the receptionist Karuna reacts upon seeing Prakash, "Oh Prakash, where were you lost? Do you know, everyone in our apartment was wishing for you." Prakash explains his reason for leaving the city and then gets to his point. "Karuna Ma'am, I am in big trouble right now, Somya Pakhawat works in your office, or, she used to work a few months ago, I need her details." Karuna says, "Oh Prakash, you won't give up your investigative habits, right? You know, the work you're talking about is very risky for me as we can't disclose the information of anyone. But still, I will do it for you, you have done a big favour for us, Prakash, if you didn't help us, people in our apartment would have died hungry during the Covid times... just wait for a while, it will take me some time to find it."

Finally, Karuna concluded her search and realized that no woman with that name had been working in that office for many years. This news seemed to put a full stop to Prakash's investigation. Then he thought why not start the investigation from a different angle? He once again requested Karuna to find out the details of Nitin Saxena, who worked in her office. Karuna was very happy, "This is a piece of cake for me, just ask me what you need to know.. but after office hours, let's meet at 6 PM at Ruposhi Bangla."

Prakash had to wait until 6 o'clock, he thought why not also get some information from Gopalan Florenza Apartment? There, when he went, he met the gatekeeper cum security Tiwari ji, who knew Prakash well. He told the whole story, he said, "Nitin Sir and Soumya Madam used to live together, I don't know if they were married or not, but they lived like husband and wife. Somya Madam was also pregnant, 2022 I don't know what happened, four or five gunmen came, and they made me and the other security guard unconscious after hearing something, later it was found out they had killed Nitin sir and taken Somya Madam with them, the case went on for many days at the police station, then Nitin sir also left from here.. what happened next, I don't know."

The lines of incomplete information were not connecting, He had to leave for Ranchi the next day because he only got a three-day leave from the office and if Prakash's boss found out the reason for the leave, he could get fired.

A little away from the apartment, there is Kuttuswami's dosa and idli shop, he doesn't understand Hindi much but he has a lot of information about the surrounding area. Prakash was also feeling hungry, so he thought of eating something and maybe he could also get some information from Kuttuswami.

After eating a masala dosa and having tea, he slowly took a chair near Kuttuswami's counter, Prakash knows a little Kannad, he started talking in Kannada, and Kuttuswami slowly opened up with Prakash when found someone talking in his language. There were few customers in the shop, so he was able to talk properly. He had never talked to Kuttuswami before. Prakash's suspicion was correct, he had a lot of information on this matter. Kuttuswami told him that Nitin and Somya's case was about religious conversion. After eating a masala dosa and having tea, he slowly took a chair near Kuttuswami's counter, Prakash knows a little Kannad, he started talking in Kannada, and Kuttuswami slowly opened up while talking in his language. There were few customers in the shop, so he was able to talk properly. He had never talked to Kuttuswami before. Prakash's suspicion was correct, he had a lot of information on this matter. He told Kuttuswami that Nitin and Somya's case was about religious conversion. According to him, maybe Somya was of the Muslim religion and without her parents' knowledge, she had changed her religion so that she could stay with Nitin, they both loved each other very much, and Somya's unknown abductors might have worked in the instructions of her parents and family.

At 6 o'clock, at Ruposhi Bangla restaurant, when Prakash met with Karuna, everything was clear. Since Karuna had a good friendship with Nitin, she knew everything about him and his love life. Nitin was deeply in love with Salma Khatoon, who was also his subordinate but Karuna could not tell what had happened to their love, the only additional information was that Nitin was working in their Pune office then of which Prakash was already aware. The whole story was clear to him now that Salma Khatoon and Somya were not two different girls, but the same person. Prakash's information was still incomplete, as he didn't know what happened to Somya, or what happened with their baby. Before leaving for Ranchi, Prakash visited Nitin's old residence, where the neighbours confirmed that Soumya, also known as Salma, had given birth to a baby girl in Sacred Oak Hospital. Finally, he called me what information along with evidential voice recordings he had collected and asked whether he needed to visit the hospital for some more information but I instructed him to come back as the collected pieces of information were enough.

On the other hand, Jannie started an investigation in Pune. Initially, Nitin had refused to meet at the office, but after much persuasion, he agreed to meet at his residence after office hours at 7:30 PM. When she arrived at his residence, she saw that he was living alone and Andy was not with him, even though the court had ordered them to stay together six months ago. Their final decision had to be made together. This was a violation of the court's instructions. When Nitin assured with conversations with Jannie that she wanted to help the couple, he agreed to give all the information as per her requirement.

Of a sudden the doorbell rang, when Nitin opened the door, Jannie's question, which surfaced in her mind then immediately floated with its answer. Andy Kar was there at the gate. She asked Nitin," Who is she? , what for has she come?" When she saw Jannie's face, she recalled and said," Yes..yes I have seen you in the first trial of our divorce case." Before Andy could say something more or Nitin could clarify something in Jannie's favour, Jannie said," Andy Madam, please listen to me faithfully, our boss Mr Rajesh Mathur uses to plead a case not only for the urge to win it, "Justice for all is the motto of all of us in our firm, ..so be calm and relax I am here to help you, you trust me and tell whatever is your agenda in married life."

Finally, I won the trust of the couple and they told me their issues turn by turn.

Andy's perspective in his words:

Our case was not a divorce case but it was made so, I don't know what happened between my father and Nitin's father, both are involved in breaking our marriage. They used to get along well, with my father, Dr. Triveny Kar, who was their family doctor, what caused the rift in the relationship, I don't know. Both are after us in such a way that we have never been allowed to spend time alone after marriage. You must be aware, since you live in Ranchi, of 'Triveny Kar Hospital'. It is the most reputed hospital in Ranchi. Virendra Sir became quite familiar to us, whenever he came for treatment, he used to stay at our place. In this way, he convinced my father to arrange my marriage with Nitin, and both fathers were happy and in agreement with the marriage proposal. I had already started liking Nitin in my heart, my M.D. was complete and suddenly our marriage was fixed. The reason was, that Nitin had told me about his love affair in Bengaluru. At first, I was shocked and wanted to rethink the marriage, but Nitin's clarity and honesty drew me towards him. I had no complaints with Nitin, the real struggle began after our marriage.

In my family my father is like Hitler, no one can dare to go against his will, at least me, he presented a case in court that Nitin is asexual, 'if that's the case then how did I become pregnant from Nitin?' Keep the husband and wife separate and challenge their masculine or feminine characteristics...where is the justice in this? I am a doctor, and I have many ways to prove that Nitin is not asexual...but for that, I have to do something in court that is not good in terms of modesty and decency. God is great, he has allowed me to meet Nitin and now pregnancy is enough for us to avoid our divorce. We want to live together, that's enough for us, we even don't to know why our fathers play such a dirty game with us.

A similar word from Nitin:

I don't know the particular intention of our fathers behind such shameful behaviour with their children, but I can smell some monetary profit motive from both of them. Even though our meetings were restricted by our father, we foolishly followed their instructions like obedient children.

Despite the circumstances that did not allow us the opportunity for togetherness, if we could go by their opinions, we still wouldn't be able to meet. We would talk to each other on the phone, even though there were not as many restrictions on us in Bengaluru. After falling in love with a Muslim girl, I was always under my father's radar, and I was unable to handle it. In such a situation, the support of a girl whom I was considering marrying, even if it was just over the phone, was incredibly lucky for me. I can't even begin to explain. All I did was that I never kept anything hidden from Andy. Even now, Andy and our meeting only happens because of a hospital project that requires Andy to come to Bombay for four or five days every month. Dr Triveny always gets Andy's room booked in advance at The Taj Hotel and stays in touch with the hotel staff by phone. With great difficulty, we managed to convince the hotel reception staff to support us, only we knew how. This way, she stays with us whenever Andy comes for 2-4 days each month. Bless those hotel staff who helped thirsty couples to reunite.

I hate my father but lack the inner strength to revolt as I know he can do any harm to me if it comes to his ego. Even the abduction of Salma, my newly born baby, could not produce enough courage within me. I alone helplessly tried to search for them, but all in vain. Finally, I had to close that chapter, of course, with the help of Andy. I proudly can say she is an exceptional girl. It is the only one who can support me in a situation in which she has been ignored and cheated by me. I finally understood the difference between love and infatuation. It was high time now to mend my mistakes. I could not lose Andy now.

Jannie listened carefully to both perspectives and took detailed notes. Finally, she said, "Before I leave, I must clarify one thing: Mr. Virendra is not responsible for the abduction of Salma and her baby. I can assure you that I will expose the intentions of Mr. Kar and Mr. Virendra behind framing your divorce case. We are almost certain of Mr. Virendra's motive, but we need valid evidence. I suspect that they are not opposing parties, as they appear to be in court. I will soon uncover their connection. You both should relax—no one can separate you now. The court will play its further role; all you need to do is attend the final hearing as scheduled."

Before leaving, Jannie took some documents from them, including a pregnancy confirmation report.

After Jannie's return, we together discussed the situation, there was now no point in wasting even the court's time.

I called Mr Jalani and said, "Sir, now there is nothing left in Nitin's divorce case, you cannot prove Nitin is asexual, and divorce will not happen this way.. it will tarnish your reputation, and I have come to know that Nitin and Andy are not living together as well if this is proven, the court's decision will not be in your favour, let's settle this out of court, it will save your reputation as well." Jalani first laughed and then said, "Rajesh, think about your reputation, I am not a novice, I have all the proof to prove Andy and Nitin's togetherness and also prove Nitin is asexual, their divorce will happen." Saying this, he disconnected his phone. Due to his reputation, he was still intoxicated today as he was when I, in the early days of my career, requested an internship under him. The way he insulted me, made fun of my LLB marks percentage and kicked me out of his office, I can never forget.

I knew that there should not be any arguments in court, and the divorce of both children should not be there at any cost. I was just worried about the intentions of my friend Virendra, I had to stand against Jalani, so that I lose and get insulted, and no matter how much I tried to defend myself, the more Nitin's false asexuality would be publicized. I had to publicize Nitin's asexuality along with their divorce as per the plans of Virendra and Kar, and for that, this time too, Virendra had made me a pawn, the first time he had put me in a dilemma in Harish's case, that time, I fought the case and I was the one who won the case but fell in my own eyes, victory was also my defeat., but this time he will not succeed in his intentions, I knew that. In this case, Nitin is sexually normal, even if there is any abnormality with any couple, this should not be the basis for divorce. Our legal system should correct the language of Section 12 of the Hindu Marriage Act 1935 so that such inability does not become the basis for divorce.

On the eve of the court hearing date, Prakash shared some information over the phone which required me to quickly arrange flights for three people from Bombay. These three people were Dr Abhishek Kundu, Sardar Bakhtawar Singh, and Mr Pawan Malhotra. It was a difficult task to get them on such short notice, as there was a fear of rejection. Half of the work had already been done by Jannie, as we already had the details of the people. Thank God, all three of them agreed to come. Now, hopefully, Virednra and Dr Kar's intentions can also be exposed.

Courtroom Drama 2:

The Ranchi High Court was like home to me, but today I felt more confident and happy because Mr. Jalani was going to be challenged in this court for the first time. The courtroom allotted for our hearing today was different from the first day of the hearing. The walls of the room suddenly almost shook ten times with the sound of the pendulum of the loud clock handing on the eastern wall, putting the whole audience in alert mode, everyone stood up, meaning it was ten o'clock and Judge Kumar was about to enter, but seeing everyone greeting him with garlands, I suddenly remembered that he was going to give the final verdict of his career, today, as he was retiring the next day. After greeting all the members, he handed the garlands to the gatekeeper and sat down for his chair, inviting everyone also to sit down, and then instructed me to begin the court proceedings.

Before going deep into the case I gave a folder of papers to the clerk to submit to the table Mr Kumar, then started,

"First of all, I would like to express my gratitude on behalf of everyone in this courtroom for the way you have consistently and honestly made your decisions during, even the difficult cases, in the lifetime commitment to justice. You, my lord, are the epitome of the entire judiciary system, and we all bow in respect before you for your contributions. My lord, I will now present some glimpses of the case before you. This is the divorce case of Nitin and Andy. In the previous hearing, a shocking incident occurred where our capable lawyer had a heart attack, but thank God, he is fine now. God bless him with good health and a long life. My lord, in difficult circumstances, you had given this couple a 6-month period of togetherness to reconsider their relationship, and they were strictly instructed to live together. In the event of unfavourable circumstances leading to a situation of living separately, it was necessary to inform the court"

I further requested Judge Kumar," My lord, I have submitted all the proofs, which are sufficient to dismiss this baseless divorce case."

" I object, my lord, how can my friend Mr Mathur, consider, this case as baseless?.. How can a sensitive lawyer condemn and disregard the clauses of the Hindu Marriage Act." appealed Jalani in a melodious voice.

Judge Kumar said," Your objection is overruled, Mr Mathur in not disregarding the law, the evidence produced by him is more than enough to dismiss this case of divorce...If you want to produce any evidence to validate your arguments, then proceed with it, else I will read the verdict as per verified pieces of evidence produced by Mr Mathur."

"My lord, I have enough pieces of evidence to prove that Nitin is asexual and his wife Andy has to go through mental trauma every night," replied Mr Jalani and his assistant produced a file on Judge Kumar's table.

I was happy that all my witnesses had arrived in time.

I requested Mr Kumar's permission to produce my witnesses in the witness box assuring him that it might help him to get the authenticity of the pieces of evidence produced by both of us

Meanwhile, Dr Abhishek Kundu's presence made Dr Kar, a little bit nervous, and called Mr Jalani's assistant to tell him something, but did not bother anything.

I first called Sardar Bakhtawawr Singh and then Mr Pawan Malhotra to the witness box. They stated that they are from The Taj, Mumbai and their work includes attending calls at the reception and passing on messages to concerned authorities. They mentioned that they had received several phone calls from Dr. Triveny Kar, who instructed them to keep an eye on his daughter, Andy Kar. They were uncomfortable when offered money and decided to record the phone conversations, which were submitted to the judge. They testified that after hearing Andy's conversation, they assisted her in meeting Nitin and that Andy never revealed her meetings with Nitin to others. When Jalani was called for cross-questioning, she refused to answer. Next, I called Dr. Kundu to the witness box, and his testimony was surprising. He revealed that he had made a deal with my father, Dr Abinash Kundu, that if he married Andy, their hospital in Bombay would collaborate with Triveny Kar Hospital. This collaboration would benefit the Lifeline Hospital in Bombay as Triveny Kar Hospital would refer their wealthy patients there. Abhishek, after learning all this, also felt it was right to support Nitin and Andy.

This time too Mr Jalani denied to cross-question the evidence.

Judge Kumar, on hearing everything said" Mr Jalani, all your evidence seems to be bogus in the light of the witnesses,...before going to read the last verdict of my law career, I give you a chance to prove your point. As all the proofs which I have been submitted by Mr Mathur are crystal clear and they prove that Nitin is sexually normal and Andy loves him "

Jalani said to the judge that he was a victim of a conspiracy and should be forgiven, and the court could now give its decision. Judge Kumar read out his verdict, "Considering the evidence and witness statements, the court reaches this decision. Nitin is normal and his wife loves him very much, therefore the court dismisses their divorce case. The court orders Mr Virendra and Dr Kar to pay a penalty of 3-3 lakhs for misleading the court and trying to prove wrong things as right. The court also instructs Jalani to refrain from filing any more cases for the next 3 months. It is ordered that Mr. Virendra and Dr. Kar explain their intentions behind the case to the court."

Virendra's intention-as told by him in the court:

"Honorable Judge and esteemed attendees, today I acknowledge all my mistakes, and, as I have just sworn on the Gita, I pledge to speak the truth. I am not like the close friend of our respected lawyer, Mr. Rajesh, whose truth and lies are hard to distinguish. Everyone knows about the great businessman of our nation, Vishesh Chhattal. It's a matter of sorrow that we have lost a patriotic son of our soil. As successful as he was in business, his personal life was equally filled with sorrow. His wife left him and formed a relationship with Uttam Shonak, the owner of the Shonak Empire, eventually marrying him. The reason she presented to the court for the divorce shattered Mr Vishesh completely and left him disheartened toward those who take pride in their masculinity or femininity. That's how he turned himself into the saviour of the LGBTQA community. His company committed itself to supporting this community, from education and livelihood to opportunities in his company. Even today, all his companies provide a 15% job reservation for this community.

From a young age, my mannerisms have been such that people often mistakenly assume I'm gay. In my days of unemployment, this manner of mine helped me rise from the ground up. Vishesh Chhattal was always dedicated to this community. I received a job offer in his company through the same reservation, though I could not medically qualify under it. But because I had won his trust, he appointed me as his bodyguard since I had some influence in the Bokaro belt. Later, I was promoted to the position of Supervisor and caretaker of one of his units at Bokaro. Mr. Chhattal trusted me so much that the company was entirely under my control."

After Chhattal Saheb's sudden death, when his will was revealed, I came up with a plan to take full ownership of our company. As disclosed in the court, I was determined to prove my son, Nitin, asexual in court. Before I learned about the will, Dr. Triveny Kar and I had decided to arrange a marriage between Andy and Nitin. Meanwhile, Nitin had grown close to his company colleague, Salma Khatoon, which posed a threat to my plan. But something happened that removed Salma from Nitin's life. Dr. Kar and I made a new agreement once again. I'm not my son's enemy; I only wanted to prove him asexual temporarily. Then, as per the will's conditions, I could meet with the board members to make Nitin the CEO, and later, I could have him marry Andy again. This way, Nitin would become a billionaire, and both of them could live a good life. Dr Kar liked my plan and agreed to it, but I had no idea that he wasn't concerned about the children—he was only interested in his gain. If you look at it, I was also thinking of my benefit, but for me, the children's happiness was more important.

I did not expect that Doctor Saheb would try to exploit the situation for his gain by joining hands with me. He wanted Andy to marry Dr Abhishek to facilitate collaborations between hospital chains. I am grateful to Abhishek, who prevented those in love from being separated.

My Lord, I have told you about all my intentions, now I request you to call Dr Kar in the witness box if the court wants to know something more about our intentions behind the case we had plotted.

With the orders of Judge Kumar, Dr Kar, came into the witness box.

Dr Kar's view, expressed by him: *My Lord, I am ashamed of my behavior. Everything Virendra Bhai shared is enough to explain our intentions to the court. Virendra Bhai's displeasure with me is justified. But regardless, we have become family, so let's forget everything and give blessings to our children. In the end, I apologize to the court once again and want to say that as long as lawyers like Mr Jalani continue proving lies as truth in court, people like us with money will continue harbouring the desire to misuse the court for our benefit. Today, I am immensely grateful to you, My Lord, for the unique verdict in the court which may be a great life lesson for me, for Virendra Bhai and Mr Jalani too. My Lord, today's final verdict of yours will be recorded in the history of the Ranchi High Court.*

Finally, Judge Kumar thanked all and concluded the procedures of the court.

Victory in this case is credited to Prakash and Jannie, and victory this time cannot be ruled out, but my mind was struck by the call of destiny. Was it a coincidence that Virendra had been charged with the same penalty amount that Harish had paid years back?

Virendra left without having a word with me as if I had made him a failure in his chronic planning.

XV
WIDOW WITH LESBIAN

Since its formation, the state of Jharkhand has embarked on an innovative initiative to gather a database for a comparative analysis of crimes in the capital. Our firm was selected to collect the data of FIRs filed in all police stations of Ranchi, along with details of court proceedings. What made this selection even more satisfying to me was the government's rejection of Mr. Jalani's firm for the same job, affirming our firm's superiority.

We were required to complete the task within a specified timeframe, prompting us to commence our work with great enthusiasm.

I was engaged in the task of reviewing the FIRs filed in 2001 at the Doranda Police Station. Amidst my review, I stumbled upon an FIR filed by Suhani Singh regarding the disappearance of a newborn girl. Suddenly, my head began to spin as memories flooded back - it was the year 2021 when Jannie entered our lives. Despite struggling to recall the specific date, I distinctly remembered the month mentioned in the FIR coinciding with the month in which Jannie joined our family. With Gourang by my side, I entrusted him with the task at hand as I hurriedly made my way to the address listed in Suhani's FIR.

I arrived at the address mentioned in the FIR and rang the doorbell, a woman came outside, and I asked "Suhani Singh used to live at this address a year ago, does she still live here?" Her answer was, "We just bought this house last year...I don't know who else, except the family from whom we bought it, used to live here before...(then pointing towards a paan shop she said)...you should ask the uncle in the paan shop ..he has been here for a long time."

I hurried to the paan shop and asked about Suhahi Singh. The shopkeeper scanned me from head to toe and said with a sly smile, "She is no more, but her companion, Jahira Begum, was quite a charmer. What elegance she carried in her movements! It seems like you are troubled as if you shared a deep bond with her in the past."

I was shocked by the news of the death of Suhani Singh, but still hopeful to get some clues from Jahira Begum.

The word used by the paan wala was making me very angry at that paan seller, but I controlled my anger and asked, "Uncle, if you know anything about him, please tell me, it's very important." He replied, "All I know is that Jahira Begum used to work in the accounting department of the narcotics department of the Jharkhand home ministry. She seemed well-educated...but...sir...she had some kind of affair with Madam Suhani...of the women...women type, although Suhani was much elder."

I said, "What nonsense are you talking about, uncle?" and then I started driving straight to the Narcotics office at Harmu. I parked the car in front of the gate and reached the accounts department to inquire about Jahira Begum. It turned out that she had already left the job. Now what should I do? I asked about her residential address from the office staff members but they refused to give me the information, citing department policy. I had no choice but to go to the department head, introduce myself, refer to the state government's database work, and eventually, after some persuasion, he allowed his PA to give me the address.

As soon as I received the address written on the slip I recalled a Hindi proverb," Bagal mei chhora aur shahar mei dhindhora."

The address written was," First Floor, Vishnu House, Namkum, Ranchi."

I was surprised that I had never seen that lady. Finally, I decided to meet her next day with Sushma as she being a lady, would be comfortable.

When I talked to Sushma about this issue at home, she said, " The dance classes in Vishnu Sound were losing their popularity so the owners sold the upper floor of the building last year; a single lady has purchased it. When the renovation was going on, I saw her, her mannerisms were different from normal women, she doesn't go out, and all her stuff is delivered online. That's all I know about her."

The night was sleepless for me, I kept getting entangled in these thoughts and questions, "Is Suhani really Jannie's mother?... Then is Virendra Jannie's father or someone else? Suhani was a widow, after all..." I kept thinking about all sorts of things. If I was thinking in the right direction then why she had thrown the newborn baby into a dustbin?

Early in the morning, my wife and I went to meet Jahira Begum. I knocked on the door for minutes but there was no response. She finally responded, "I have ordered nothing and don't want to meet anyone." I said, "Please, open the door. I have to meet you to talk about Suhani." At first, she refused to meet us, but after many requests, she agreed and invited us inside. She said, "I won't ask you how you found out about me, but Suhani was my love. My life has become difficult without her. I know how I have been living without her for so many months. I couldn't concentrate even on my job, so I quit the job. She was much older than me but she was my life."

Her words seemed strange to Sushma because she was talking about the love between two women as if it were the love between a husband and wife. But I had studied a lot about lesbians, so it was normal for me, and I had respect for her feelings. When Jahira saw the bewildered face of Sushma, she abruptly said, "I don't have any shame to inform you that I am a lesbian."

A few months ago, I didn't know what lesbians were, so the only term I learned for the whole community of third genders was "Hijra." Sushma was really unware of the term 'lesbian'.

She continued, "As per the record of my job profile in the Narcotics department, I am a female and in my Aadhar records too, as before 2014 there was no provision of mentioning 'third gender' in such records in India. This was also one of the reasons for leaving my job. My ways revealed that I am different from the normal female. Many in my office used to see me with different eyes as if I were a criminal. What could I do? There were no parameters then, in front of me that would help me in proving my gender identity."

I consoled her, "In today's scenario, third-gender members are no less capable than males or females. They are appointed for all types of jobs and respected in society. Since 2019, they are eligible to get their identity certificates from DM offices in India."

She was not very satisfied with my consolation and said, "Sir, getting a rule passed in India and its strict observation are two different things. To get proper respect, we still have to go for miles. Changing the mindset of people regarding the third-gender community is the need of the hour. That will bring true justice to our community. Otherwise, we will continue to be tossed among the surfaces of disrespectfulness, funny creatures, and mysterious sex. No families feel proud to introduce our community to their kids. Sir, we live under various dogmas and humiliation, so please leave this matter separate and come to your actual point."

Sushma was unable to become frank with Jahira. Still, I respectfully kept my query in front of Jahira," I need information regarding Suhani's death,..., the birth of her child and the event of missing her newly born baby, for a legal purpose.

She said," I don't know, for what legal purpose you need this information, still I will tell you everything, as you know the third eye of one, belonging to the third gender community, is more active than normal people,...and I can see,...you people are innocent."

Suhani's story by Jahira:

Suhani was a victim of child marriage, at the age of 14 she married Shekhar Singh from a Zamindar family who was much older than her, they had a difference of 20 years of age. At that early age, she faced severe sexual torture from her husband still she was trying to adjust ,after two years of married life Sekhar was murdered by a member of his hostile family. Suhani became a widow, and in their community widow remarriages were prohibited in those days so she had to come back to her father's home. A few years later there blossomed love in her life, a student named Virendra, living in the adjoining building fell in love with her. Without knowing each other's past that Suhani was a widow and Virendra was already married, their love started to flourish. Before the entry of a father as a villain into the love story, one of Virendra's fast friend acted the role of a villain and succeeded in separating the love buds. But love can not be imprisoned. A few years later the lovers met again and spent a week in the Sisai Hotel. Now there was entry of the real villain , Suhani's father Munna Singh, into the love story, changed the game. Virendra was taken into police custody for abducting Suhani. Munna Singh imprisoned her daughter in a room as we can watched in 90's Hindi movies. One of her younger brother, Amar, came to know that his sister was pregnant, and he helped Suhani to escape from prison. Many nights she spent on railway platforms without food. She was free from her father's prison but there were many challenges in front of her. Father's fear,..hunger. lack of den to hide herself.

One day by chance her hidden beauty caught my eye, and I fell in love with her, she was much older than me but it was my first love and third for her. We spent beautiful moments together for months but the birth of her baby changed our lives drastically. Suhani hated Virendra so much that he did not come forward to notice her pain. She always thought the baby was a symbol of the cheater Virendra. One late night when I was not at home, she threw the baby in a dustbin near a red light at Lalpur. It was her instant act under some bad emotions, soon when she realised about her deed she rushed to the place but the baby was not there. When I came back, we immediately went to Doranda Police Station to lodge an FIR for the loss of the child. After that, she almost lost her mental status, her guilt was killing her day by day. I was committed to her love, and I tried to provide all care but she could not survive, the guilt within her took her life one day and I lost my love. This is my love story with Suhani, what information more can I provide to you..?

During the whole story Sushma and I were only thinking of our beloved Jannie but I could not reveal her identity as it could adversely affect Jannie and her parents. But everything was crystal clear to us. There was a curiosity in my mind so while departing I asked," Could Suhani's brother have helped her differently? "

In this Jahira said," As I had come to know that that was a part plan of Munna Singh to get rid of her daughter and the infamy related to Suhani's pregnancy."

She added," The worst part of Suhani's faith in Virendra was that when she tried to contact him, after leaving Munna Singh's home, at the address which was provided to her, she found that the address was wrong."

As soon as we came to our house Sushma was getting emotional about the sufferings of little Jannie but I sent a voice message to Virendra through WhatsApp,

"Virendra, our past meetings were not so memorable, Nitin's case made everything worse, but I wish to give you an offer of remorse for cheating on Suhani, don't worry she has gone to heaven leaving your daughter behind, my concern is Suhani's friend who belongs to the LGBTQA community. She might be a solution for your company's heir. I think God has allowed you an opportunity to wash out your bad karma. If you like my suggestion, you can meet me at my home but remember one thing,....you will get no clue about your daughter. One more thing, Suhani's friend is a female in her official records, some legal documentations are required to get her original identity as lesbian, if you like you can take services of my firm in this regard"

XVI
ANGRY YOUNG-MAN

I was sitting in my office, going through the details of a case on my laptop a suddenly the voice of Gourang distracted me from my concentration. "May I come in, sir?" he asked. I replied, "Yes, come in." Adding, "Sit down, the angry young man." Gourang responded shyly, "Sir, you are pulling my leg." He then asked, "Sir, may I take a few minutes of your precious time?"

I reassured Gourang, "My son, don't be formal, sit and say whatever you want to." He then emotionally expressed, "Sir, you never behaved like a boss with your subordinates, you are a fatherly figure to all of us in this firm. Still, I misbehaved with you and blamed you for giving special favour to Jannie." Gourang continued, "Sir, I have realized now that you have always been right. Jannie is more talented, her contributions to the firm are immense, and she deserves everyone's appreciation. Please forgive me for my rude behaviour."

I was impressed by Gourang's change of heart towards Jannie and responded, "Gourang, I have always valued everyone's viewpoints during meetings. Your expressions of anger were okay with me as they were your opinions. I only intervene when someone's attitude and behaviour could be harmful to the firm. So, don't worry about these trivial matters and focus on your job." I comforted him and he left my cabin.

Reflecting on the sudden change in Gourang's behaviour, I couldn't help but sense a mild fragrance of love for Jannie in his heart. I couldn't conclude without valid evidence, so I decided to play a trick to clarify my thoughts. Closing my eyes for a few seconds and reopening them, I found Jannie standing in front of me. At that moment, I exclaimed, "Eureka, eureka!" Jannie looked puzzled and asked, "What eureka, sir?" I smiled and replied, "The truth, Jannie, the truth!" I kept asking, "Jannie.. What is your opinion about Gourang?" Jannie had a hesitant reaction, but still asked in a low voice, "Why, Sir?" I said just like that. She started speaking, "He is a very good boy.. honest.. but due to his circumstances, he behaves rudely sometimes.. something has happened in his life that makes someone's soul tremble when they hear about it.

"Jannie,..I want to hear everything about him,...if you know." I said. At the same time the doubt in my mind about their love blossoming had taken the path of truth and the story was becoming clearer, as no one in the except her knew the critical circumstances of Gourang's life.

Gourang's past life, as told by Jannie:

Bishnupur, in the Bankura district, is a town known for its small temples. Located in the lap of nature, this beautiful town is filled with natural beauty. On Ramakrishna Road in

Bishnupur, there is an old mansion belonging to a wealthy individual, Shri Krisnapada Mazumdaar, Gourang Mazumdar's father. He had lost his glory for his gambling habit and now farming was his only source of income. He had entrusted his land for cultivation to Samata Dutta. After losing wealth, prosperity and fame KrishnaPada became addicted to liquor which used to be out of his control all the time, in this situation, Shyamali Mazumdar, his wife, has to look after their household needs, cultivation and everything

Samanta Dutta was a healthy, muscular and trustworthy man of about 50 years, he lost his wife years back during COVID-19.

Samanta was the right hand of Shyamali Mazumdar so they usually had meetings regarding household matters. During that Durga Puja, the atmosphere was filled with the sounds of drums and celebrations all around as usual at Bishnupur. The smell of incense and smoke was intoxicating the entire city.

Gourang had decided to stay at Shyam Bazar Law College, hostel, this time during pooja, as he had heard very highly about the grand celebration of Durga Puja in Kolkata. but destiny decided something else, Gourang was called home by someone in an emergency, so he quickly caught the Ruposhi Bangla Express train and reached home in a hurry. On one side, preparations for the farewell of Goddess Durga were in full swing at the main worship pandal of Ramakrishna Road, while on the other side, the procession of Shyamli Mazumdar's body was being taken out from the old, grand and majestic building of Krishna Pada. The priest of the puja pandal said that taking the idol of Durga Maa through that route on which the body of Shyamali was to be carried, was inauspicious and instructed to take the arthi through a different route, leading to the cremation ground. Following the instructions, both processions were carried out, but fate had other plans. Both processions met at a crossroads, with the Trishul of Durga Maa's idol piercing the chest of a demon Mahishasur, now for some reason straightened towards people as if the Goddess were to throw it toward the real culprits of the death of the lady. People started to talk that it was a bad omen for the future of the city but some people concluded to have a solution and the procession of the dead body was moved first and then Ganga water was sprinkled on the road before Durga Maa's idol was to be moved ahead for immersion in the flowing water. Tears seemed to flow from Durga's idol during immersion as well, whether they were tears of farewell or tears for the woman being falsely accused, was unclear.

Everyone was shocked, no one was prepared to console Gourang or explain to him what had happened to his mother. His father was always lost in intoxication. He had grown up now and had developed the capacity to endure pain. He cremated his mother and fulfilled all the rituals, but it seemed as if his voice had left him, he had stopped speaking. Gradually, he had felt everything. His grandmother had accused his mother of having an inappropriate relationship with Samanta Dutta. Gourang's alcoholic father had also supported his mother and Shyamali Mazumdar could not bear it as she was in touch with Samanta due to his husband's ply from responsibilities, this blame by his husband made no option for her except to take her own life.

Life is such a strange thing that takes years to handle, but a vial of poison can end it in a moment. The worst part was that the poison for him was arranged by his alcoholic father himself.

Gourang was not feeling good in Bisnupur after all the rituals had taken place. He had decided to go back to Kolkata. His mother used to manage his expenses in Kolkata, and now he had to do it all by himself. He had thought about tutoring children in Kolkata because he had no hope from his alcoholic father. Although his sister Arundhati and brother-in-law Kundan had assured him of bearing his expenses. Before leaving, he thought it was appropriate to meet Uncle Samanta. But meeting him changed his whole world. He was very sad and said, "Your mother was beautiful both inside and out," Samanta's words pierced Gourang like an arrow. Although he and Arundhati also used to say something similar about her. Praising the beauty of his mother was something different he was startled when he heard about it from Samanta so he left. He came to Kolkata and started an inner battle. He started to feel that his mother was wrong. His father and grandmother seemed right to him. For almost a year, he kept fighting within himself, one day by chance he met Samanta in Bara Bazar of Kolkata, he didn't want to talk at first but talking he found out that he suffered some side effects of vaccination of Covid19 and he was being treated by Kolkata's famous psychiatrist Dr Sukumar Saha. He said that he had been suffering from the mental trauma of the disease for two years. He further explained that his disease can not be cured but he wants to come out of the trauma. Neither Samanta told what the disease was nor Gourang asked about it. After a few days when he Googled about Dr Sukumar Saha of Kolkata, he was shocked. He was a pioneer in treating the males psychologically who had become impotent due to some accident. The impotent males always have to suffer a lot of mental pressure and they fight internal battles, Dr Saha helps them to get rid of their mental burden to live in society without any sense of guilt.

Gourang had realized clearly that the COVID vaccination had made Samanta impotent, who could not be cured now. He just wanted to overcome the mental trauma of losing his masculinity and was fighting a different battle in life, but society left no stone unturned to suppress him and toss his name with Gourang's mother. In the process of habitual lying to some people for fun, sprinkled black ink on the character of his mother and helplessly she had to lose her life. Gourang was filled with hatred towards all these things, particularly himself, for tarnishing his mother's character. Consumed by these thoughts, he became immersed in feelings of disgust and day by day, his behaviour changed in such a way,

I was very much sad for poor Gourang, and told Jannie, "What pain had he hidden in his heart!"

Jannie said," Sir, he is a good and innocent fellow and dedicated to his job but his past life has made his nature a little rebellious." She continued," He can not bear an injustice and lies spoken by someone for fun,.. whether it is in the legal procedures or the society,.. two days ago he had some hot talks with a drunken police constable because he threw his lathi on a poor rickshaw puller without any reason, ..other policemen came making fun of him started alleging him falsely, in support of the drunken constable, ..for God shake I was with him and managed the situation."

Janies's remark, shaked me from inside," Actual cause of death of Shyamali Aunty was actually a lie spoken by one of her neighbourer , simply for fun."

Any way, listening to everything from Jannie made me aware of their calculus of heart.

Now it was my turn to talk to De Souza's about their togetherness, hoping I could convince them.

I was sure that Sushma would be extremely happy to hear this news of budding romance.

XVII
YOU TUBE MANIA

Nowadays, social media has taken over people's lives, causing them to become distant from their families. People don't have time for each other because they are always on YouTube or Facebook. The loneliness that already exists in nuclear families . India has been exacerbated by social media taking over people's lives. This is a topic for thought and discussion - has social media given us more or taken more from us? Have the founders of these platforms brilliantly exploited people's vulnerabilities for their business gains?

Once I came across a video on YouTube, on the topic,' How to get rid of YouTube addiction,' and it had almost twenty lakh views.

Sushma too is not an exception, she spends a good deal of time watching various channels on YouTube platform. She likes religious videos to watch, her favourite one is an interview channel on Christianity.

Today I think, if we had the kind of social exposure in our college days, which can make an ordinary person special overnight, daily we see the births of new mahatmas by making videos go viral, then maybe Harish would have become a great saint and leader today, with millions of followers and who knows what else. Only one fan, Jaskirat Singh had made him a 'Divyatma' and so popular in Ranchi that he had developed hundreds of real followers, I am still confused whether his situation then was the actual call of destiny or a fake one.

I know Harish enough to know that he has no regrets about leaving behind that illusionary life, instead, he has left that glamour behind, and he is happy with his simple life now.

One day when I came home from court I found Sushma busy watching her favourite Christian channel on YouTube. The sound volume on the mobile phone is somehow high as she was not using earphones.

The first time I came to know the name of her favourite channel. " Memories of Father Christopher with Monk Philip". " Father Christopher"..I exclaimed..., tried to recall.. within a minute I collected the memory of the Cathedral where Harish used to go to meet Father Christopher. I got excited but without disturbing Sushma I thought to browse the channel and watch it when I had time. The next day I started to scroll YouTube on my mobile phone in the office. All of a sudden, I came across a video, on the channel where Monk Philip was describing the confessions of a math PG student, which caught my attention. I shared the link on my other mobile phone if you lose a video for any reason on U-tube, it takes lots of time to search for it again. I started watching from the beginning

Monk Philip's words on the channel:
I am your friend, Philip, and you are watching "Memories of Father Christopher by Monk Philip." In this show, I highlight the lives of some people from Father's Diary who acknowledged

their mistakes and sincerely tried to rectify them, serving as a source of inspiration for all of us. As you know, we do not reveal the names of individuals in this program. Names of individuals in my programme are always A,B,C....Today, we will draw inspiration from Mr A. Before moving forward, I want to express my heartfelt gratitude to all of you for liking and supporting the program. It brings me great joy to inform you that we now have over 500,000 subscribers. Please continue to shower us with your love and support. Today, I will share the struggles of a young man from Father's diary, who bravely fought his inner battles.

Mr. A was a mathematics PG student. He had always been frustrated since childhood, craving love from his family. His elder brother was so talented that his parents never even acknowledged his existence, as he was not so intelligent . To gain attention in college, he started spreading rumors about having a girlfriend in another city, using lies and false evidence. This tactic started working for him. He started becoming quite popular among his friends in college. He started enjoying the attention of people. And thus begins the story of his inner conflict.

The story was progressing with lies reaching its peak, now he was running out of evidence to support his claims so he ended his love story by killing his imaginary lover. But the opposite happened, everyone sympathized with him. The appearance of the deceased lover in his dream was the next twist in the story as if he had performed a miracle. Standing in support of a family when Indira Gandhi was assassinated and riots broke out in the Sikh community, he began to be seen as a saint. Along with his good deeds, like teaching the neighbourhood children for free, taking someone to the hospital if someone in their family fell ill, helping someone with government work, and going to meetings, all of these made him famous as a saint overnight. His sermons were being organized in the alleys and streets. It was good for him, but all of this started to get a little excessive.

His friend had gotten him into a situation where he had to continue with his lie. The internal conflict forced him to face the truth, and that is when he met Father Christopher. The Father listened to all he had to say and explained, "There is a fine line between lying and deceit, it is not wrong for a person to use deceit for the greater good of others for a short time. However, one should never cross the boundary of deceit and enter the realm of lies, always keep this in mind".

Mr A said, "Father, in the lectures in which I get invited to speak, I have to read countless books and study various religious texts to speak."

The Father smiled and said, "Son, acquiring knowledge about religion is important. However, the real importance lies in the knowledge that we hold in our hearts. By reading religious scriptures, we gain knowledge of the right path, but to put that knowledge into practice, we must have religious faith and devotion in our hearts. Therefore, not only does reading books make us truly religious, but also having the ability to follow it. And I must say these sermons and their preparations will certainly help you in reaching the apex of humanity. Our life is a journey to transform our soul into a divine spirit and merge it with the Almighty. The Supreme Being has given us everything; around us lies the spark of knowledge, like a matchstick, and within us, our soul is like a candle. All we need is to strike the matchstick against the surface of gunpowder and ignite the wick of the candle with the spark. The light of knowledge will then be ready to illuminate our soul. " "In this way, Mr A started to meet the Father whenever he needed. Once my father said, 'Believe in Gandhi ji or not but try to look at the world through his perspective, you will never choose the wrong path.'The story of Gandhi ji in which a mother complained to him that her son eats a lot of jaggery, he called the boy's mother after 15 days and when she again came with the chid after 15 days, he simply told the child not to eat jaggery. The mother did not like Gandhi ji's behaviour and said, "Bapu, if you had to say this much, why didn't you say it when we came 15 days ago, why did you bother us again?" To this, Gandhi ji replied that he used to eat jaggery himself, but he has stopped the addiction of eating it in these 15 days. Now only I have right to instruct or advise it to the child. This story that Mr. A had heard from Father Christopher, brought a significant change in A's life, and he decided to eliminate the darkness within himself. He slowly began to move away from a bad habit of telling lies for cheap publicity and joined the struggle of transforming himself. He had well understood that becoming great is simpler than becoming a simple human being. The glamours of publicity had seemed now to be a trivial matter to him. What happened next in Mr A's life, did he manage to overcome his inner darkness, did he become a great saint, to know all this, stay tuned for part 2 of this video. Until then, thank you all for watching the video. And if you are new to the channel, do not forget to subscribe.

The perspectives of the inner struggles of Harish were not very shocking to me. still, I was thinking, if only back then social media was like this and I had come across this video, then I wouldn't have been caught in a strange dilemma during my first ever court case at the beginning of my career.

XVIII

ROADS CROSSED AND ROADS LOST

Harish was married to Ratna, who was beautiful, cultured, and educated. Before the marriage, Ratna laid down a condition with Harish. She said, "I've come to know about rumours regarding your past life affairs, and I want nothing to do with hidden truths or surprises, if there's anything in your past, I want you to be completely open—your words should be clear and pure, as honest as milk but if anything undisclosed comes to light, that day will be the last for us and don't take these words as a routine and simple warning from a wife." Harish had explained everything to Ratna and assured her that he would tell the truth about everything concerning himself and that he did not have any affair with anyone. Due to trust and honesty, a different kind of bond was forming between them and their love for each other was growing stronger, day by day.

The growing intensity of their love often left me troubled by one recurring thought—Harish's two dreams that came to him at night. One was of a train, and the other was of Sudha appearing in his dream. I kept praying to God that these dreams would not affect their married life.

Ratna was encountered by his dream of train passing the tunnel for two three times , till I lived in Delhi and they had thought some plan to way out. They lived for each other and these issues could not easily shake the their strong bond , and I loved seeing that. Their love touched my heart. If they were like Ram and Sita, I always wanted to play the role of Hanuman in their lives. This Ramayana of us is different from the divine one. In the original, Laxman left Urmila for 14 years without any selfish motive. But here, Virendra separated from Anita and Suhani for a year and a half, driven by his self-interest. And when his desires went unfulfilled, he abandoned his brother. The situations that arose in life would often remind me, effortlessly, of the time during our school days when we participated in a play of the Ramayana. Truly understanding Ram isn't easy—only someone as divine as Lord Shiva or as devoted to Shiva as Ravana can do so. But if one wishes to hold Sita and Ram within their heart, then Hanuman's path is the way. The memory of that day is still clear in my mind, how he brought his wife Ratna to Delhi after their wedding and how I had decorated our rented house in Nimri Colony, as we had already shifted from Mukherji Nagar to this place just after Virendra had left Delhi. It felt like a celebration and for me, entering Ratna into Harish's life was no less than a festival. During those days, mobile phones were not common, so the trend of taking photos on mobile phones was less. I had gifted them a beautiful camera of the Yashika Company brand, a pride back then. They used to go out together in Delhi, and I would act as their photographer, feeling like the third wheel. Since I wasn't married at the time, I didn't understand that a newlywed couple needs privacy and I always used to be bones in the kebabs. But it was the best part of my life that Ratna always appreciated all my gestures like those. Our life was going great, I was happy in the happiness of the couple, Harish would go for his daily office duties, I would go to college for my law classes and sometimes study at home when classes were cancelled, helping Ratna in the kitchen. I always saw Ratna as my sister. That's why I was always eager to help her. But this fact bothered the neighbours, they started gossiping about me and Ratna. When Harish would come home from the office in the evening, sometimes Sardar Sukhwinder Singh's wife would say, "Harish- Bhai Saheb, your friend just stays at home, has his law college people kicked him out?" Harish understood her gestures but chose to ignore them. I had faced the suspicious eyes many a time but ignored them. Ultimately I had decided, that I should rent a separate house, this could be the solution to the situation and to shut the mouths of people up. When I talked to them about it, Ratna said, "Rajesh Bhaiya, this is our life, not the neighbours'... why should we bring changes in our life because of others, you will stay here with us, this is what I want ...the rest you and Harish decide." In the end, I came up with a solution to leave home with Harish, whether there was a class or not, and study in the library and come back after the arrival of Harish from the office. But soon I had to change my decision. It happened that one day we both left home and reached our respective destinations. After going to my faculty, I discovered that I didn't bring the project work and today was the last submission date. Nimri Colony is very near to North Campus, I took an autorickshaw and came back home but what saw there, changed my priority, Ratna was screaming in stomach pain but no one was there to help her, I rushed her to the doctor and brought her home after treatment, and promised to stay together so that we could help each other in times of trouble. I thought to let the people keep saying, whatever they wished, I knew myself and my intentions well.There were only a few months left for my course to be completed and the final exams to be held. Now I had to study at home and only go to college during class time. Thinking about how everything changes with time? ..my eyes are getting moist, now. How everything has become a bit mechanical? There is some fault of mine in this and the first case I fought for Virendra is equally responsible. After completing the course, I came to Ranchi and fought the first case against Harish for Virendra. I won the case, which was good for my career, but my victory was a loss of 3 lakh to Harish as a penalty posed by the court, who had already spent lakhs on Virendra. And if I had lost, Harish and Ratna's marriage would have broken as per conditions laid by Ratna before marriage. My victory in my first case was not a major achievement of my life, but it would have been better if another lawyer should have fought this case. I, sometimes feel guilty for fighting the case of Virendra against Harish. Virendra has always been responsible for putting me in such a dilemma where I can not decide about the case whether I should fight it to lose or to win.

Before leaving Delhi, Virendra had a big fight with Harish. He had asked once again thank Harish to take a loan of 3 lakh rupees,, from LIC to start his business, otherwise, he had threatened to ruin Harish but he was helpless and could not do that as it was a huge sum of money, and it would have taken him years to repay the loan. But Harish had said, "I'll arrange for a job as an LIC agent by speaking at the office. Gradually, you'll rise, and you'll start earning well. You will see this job be your jumping pad to touch the sky." Virendra adamantly replied," I am fading up with your fake promises, fake calls in the name of destiny. I want to see results..immediate results, I have wasted one and a half years believing in such promises and dreams and past life complications." Becoming helpless he somehow managed to arrange 50 thousand rupees before leaving. Virendra was not happy till the end and left after threatening to ruin Harish. Then he struggled for a year in his home city for business, got frustrated and then filed a false case against Harish to destroy his career and a claim of Rs. 3 lacks was made for this loss.

He had an obsession, almost madness, to become a big man, but without hard work or devoting the time needed. He never realized that fruit only turns sweet when it ripens at the proper desired time. In our lives, sometimes we come across a road which may lead us to our destination but we lose the road due to various reasons and thoughts. Gain and loss, correct or incorrect are nothing but the outcomes of our thought process. Avdhoot Baba Shivanand ji says, "Choose a path with a feeling of gratitude for every person and everything, and start your journey, you will surely reach your destination. "As a lawyer today, I feel that I won the case in favour of Virendra, but if I think as a friend, it seems like I betrayed Harish by fighting the case for Virendra. And if I think from Ratna's perspective, it feels like a brother's victory. I too was swayed by Virendra and started believing Harish was wrong. In this way, I supported the wrong. Since I value friendship in all relationships, I always accept my defeat in this case.

XIX

A REUNION IN DELHI; UNSPOKEN HOPES

A special type of police conference was organized in Delhi by the Home Ministry, where police inspectors and higher officers from each state were invited as representatives. The conference focused on various issues such as the Naxalite problem, the societal perspective on the LGBTQA community and discrimination, counselling for adolescent males to prevent the increasing number of rapes, etc. Pranab was also invited because his police station was in a Naxalite region, and he had successfully resolved a case involving a transgender person. It was a good opportunity, and we all planned a trip to Delhi. There were many reasons for this. I had never met Harish's children before, and neither Harish nor Ratna had met my family members.

Although at this time, my meeting with Harish's children was not possible, we could meet only with Srijan, not with Shavy. Harish and I wanted to resolve the differences between us, and it would also allow Sushma and Ratna to meet. So far, both families have only been connected through mobile phones.

Ratna had specifically told me over the phone that we all had to stay at their house, Sushma and I were ready to stay with them, but arrangements were made for Pranav to stay in a hotel by the Jharkhand Police Department. and he had to stay there. When we reached New Delhi station by Ranchi Rajdhani Express and unboarded the coupe of the compartment, I found Ratna and Harish waiting on the platform to receive us, it was a great moment to meet my friend after so many years. Harish and I were sitting in the front seat of the car, while Ratna and Sushma were sitting in the back seat. Harish was driving the car and we were talking about random things, but the two in the back seat were chatting as if they were long-lost friends, even though they were meeting for the first time. They have a big bungalow in New Friends Colony. They had invested their large amount of hard-earned money in the bungalow, a big bungalow with a garden in the front space which was beautifully managed, and a variety of flowers, especially many species of roses enhanced the beauty of the garden. I was quite mesmerised at the first look at their house.

As I looked at the rose bushes in the garden, suddenly I thought, "I wish Pranav had come here, he would have enjoyed it a lot, but he had already taken a taxi from the station to The Lalit Hotel as destined earlier.

As soon as we crossed the lawn area a sweet and beautiful girl almost 21-22 years came to greet us, I understood she was Srijan. Harish usually talked about

Shavy and Srijan over the mobile phone but never shared their photographs.

Srijan's behaviour, her ways of talking, and her politeness, all left their imprints in my heart. She took us to our room where we were to stay. We took a bath and got fresh after that Srijan came and said," Rajesh uncle and Sushma aunt, lunch is ready. Dad and Mom are waiting at the table, for you to join. We enjoyed the delicious lunch and then sat in the drawing room. Srijan prepared the chart for all seven days of our stay in Delhi, including where to visit on which day. In today's schedule, Harish and I had to go for a long drive. Ratna and Sushma were scheduled to visit Akshardham Temple with Srijan. "A perfect planning-loneliness for old friends", I said and appreciated Srijan's IQ. I then talked with Srijan on various topics, one of her logical cum mathematical discussions amazed me and I became a fan of her intelligence.

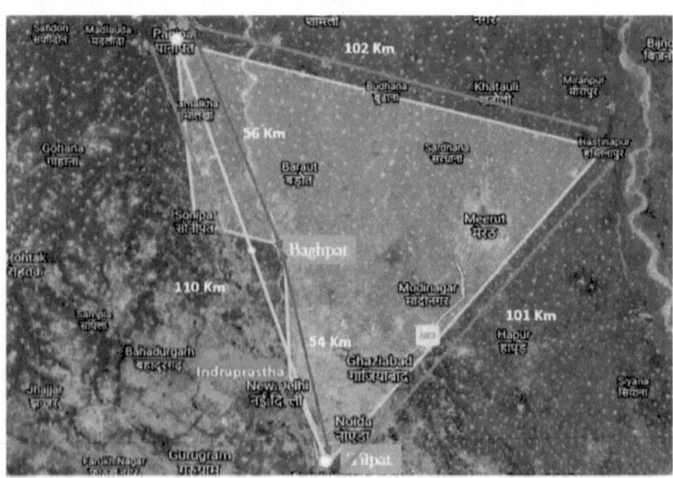

Photo of five villages demanded by Krishna for Pandavas during negotiation before war

She explained to me why Lord Krishna demanded the five villages for Pandavas mentioned below, during peace negotiations:

Indraprastha: Also known as Delhi, this was the capital of the Pandavas' kingdom

Swarnprastha: Also known as Sonipat

Panprastha: Also known as Panipat

Vyaghrprastha: Also known as Baghpat

Tilprastha: Also known as Tilpat

The prosperity of these villages was insignificant compared to their unique mathematical configurations. They formed a triangular region, which is known to be the strongest structure in geometry. Krishna believed that with the combined strength of these five villages, the Pandavas would be able to expand their empire as far as they desired. Srijan asserted that the idea was entirely her own. She said to me," I have the book- ' Is God a Mathematician?'-by Mario Livio, I have read it, at least fifty times and from then I find a mathematical angle at every act or creation of God." I could neither deny her philosophy nor support it without any proof from the scriptures but I could sense the par excellence in her thoughts. Her way of thinking was based on a unique combination of religion, mathematics and logic.

Suddenly, I remembered something Sushma once told me Pranav had told her that he was never a good student in math, so he would marry a girl who could use mathematical and logical thoughts in day-to-day life, because this way the next generation would be good at mathematics. Today, mathematics is the future.

According to the plan made by Srijan, Harish and I went for a long drive and Srijan booked an Uber for the three of them to visit Akshardham Temple.

This time I was in the driver's seat because on a long drive, we weren't concerned about road ideas, just about driving. Harish was going to drive on the way back, and I had some idea about the roads, but in all these years, Delhi's roads have completely changed. The entire face of Delhi has changed. When we came to Delhi for studies, it was just after the Asian Games were organized and Delhi had changed completely. So many flyovers and roads were built. We were amazed when we first came to Delhi, with all its hustle and bustle, but today Delhi's hustle and bustle is something else.

As soon as we crossed New Friends Colony and approached the red light, the car had to stop. I saw an old man shouting and cursing Sumit loudly. I was surprised. Seeing my astonishment, Harish explained, "He's mad. People say that this man and Sumit Jhalar were very close friends. They had a business partnership, but it's said that Mr. Jhalar took over the entire business and threw him out. Since then, he's gone mad and keeps cursing Sumit." I was troubled by the thought of such betrayal. I said, "How wonderful it would be if, like computers, our brains had a 'delete' button, which can help in removing browsing history in internet—at least people wouldn't suffer these fits of madness." Harish replied," No, Raaj, you can't delete your internet browsing history completely, it can still be found in 'System restore,' in 'Internet cookies', 'Desktop search program'," and who knows from where all this can be traced?" While driving from New Friends Colony via Badarpur Border, we reached Faridabad. On the way, we did not talk much about ourselves and instead discussed the development of Delhi. While driving on the road of Sector 51, we saw a market on the left side that looked like a foreign market, named World Street. The beauty of the market forced me to stop the car. I parked the car and both of us headed towards the market. Harish was also visiting this market for the first time, and it felt like we had entered a market in Paris. Harish suggested going for tea somewhere, so we searched for a tea shop. After some searching, we found a shop named 'Tea Trends'. We entered the shop and sat down. The menu had more than 20 varieties of tea. We were confused about which variety to order, but then we saw a variety named 'God's Tea' on the menu and decided to order that due to its divine name. While waiting for our tea, we chatted and I praised Srijan's IQ and mathematical skills. He said, "Since childhood, she has been good at math and has unwavering faith in the Hindu religion, especially in Lord Shiva. But let me tell you, his qualities have also become her troubles to all of us." Harish became sad as he said this and continued further, "Srijan used to worship Lord Shiva for hours,... when she reached puberty, during her menstrual cycle, going to the temple and performing rituals was prohibited according to our traditions, ,... this made Srijan sad, and she prayed to God that her cycle would stop forever so she could worship Shiva continuously and that's exactly what happened—her menstrual cycle stopped from the following month onward,.. since the age of 15, our daughter's cycle has stopped,... as her parents, Ratna and I are deeply concerned about her condition, though she is content and finds happiness in her devotion to Lord Shiva,.. we've tried numerous medical treatments, but none have yielded results,...in medical terms, this condition is similar to' amenorrhea'. However, despite all possible tests and examinations, the doctors have not been able to pinpoint the cause, as her symptoms differ entirely from those of both primary and secondary amenorrhea. Srijan, however, believes this to be a divine blessing from God. She willingly supports the medical treatments, if only to reassure us, and has a remarkable ability to connect scientific facts with spiritual insights—or explain religious concepts through science."I had come to know all of Srijan's qualities in just one day, especially the logical and mathematical explanation he gave for Krishna's request for five specific villages for the Pandavas before the Kurukshetra war. But I was stunned; the thought of his illness kept circling in my mind. Just then, "God's tea" was served to us. I was surprised—it was just simple green tea. The bill for it was more surprising, it was Rs 500. What a business; putting a catchy name to the common thing and serving it stylishly could price at 100x!Both were dissatisfied with the tea, that came out.I was thinking about how people manage to do all kinds of business these days... The importance of product quality in making a business flourish is decreasing day by day; all that matters now is that the publicity should be attractive. This time Harish took the driver's seat and we drove to Badkhal Lake. After reaching Badkhal Lake, the beauty of nature gave us great relief which helped our brains switch from the disease of Srijan."On the way back, I asked Harish, 'Have you talked to Sarvesh Bhaiya about Srijan's illness? He's an expert in this kind of disease, after all."Harish replied, "Yes, initially, he provided online consultations for a year, but there was no significant change. Later, he referred the case to Dr. Lithardo, who is now the head of the research unit at Massachusetts General Hospital in Boston. This research centre in Boston, Massachusetts is the largest medical research centre in the world. The good thing is that Sarvesh Bhaiya's son, my nephew, Dr. Sampat Raajdaan, is conducting research under him. Their research is also somewhat related to Srijan's condition, as he is studying how a very high IQ level affects a person's meiosis process. Srijan has been receiving some placebo treatment (as her disease has no sure cure with medical science) from Dr Lithardo online mode for five years, but there hasn't been much improvement. I was a little bit confused as I didn't know what it was so at my query Harish simplified, "Many studies have found a small to moderate negative correlation between IQ and fertility rates. However, these studies have been limited US and some European countries. Common people have IQ levels between 85 and 115 but having IQ levels more than 130 tells about someone having an extraordinary brain. It is said that to date Albert Einstein had the highest IQ level i.e. 160. It 142 in the case of Srijan."I have never thought that a high IQ level of someone might be fatal.After returning home, I asked Sushma about her visit to Akshardham at night. I found out that she enjoyed it, especially the light and fountain show, which she found wonderful. But more than the visit, she kept praising Srijan. She said, "The entire garden in front of this house is maintained by Srijan... she has a deep love for roses... Rajesh, couldn't we find someone like Srijan for our son, Pranav?"I could understand what was going in the mind of Sushma, which provoked me to discuss Srijan's disease. Still, Sushma had no issues, she said," We should give Pranav this proposal, and let him decide."According to Srijan's plan, we all continued exploring Delhi together. As per the itinerary, our last day included a visit to the PM Museum, which everyone thoroughly enjoyed. Harish and I even took a selfie with Pandit Nehru. While visiting together, I remembered my role as a photographer during my law college days. Today the role was being played by Srijan but one thing was still the same, it was the chemistry between Ratna and Harish. The days spent in Delhi, were some very special days in our lives, refreshing many old memories. After sharing so many memories, we took our leave from there. On the return journey, as scheduled, Pranav met us at the station.

For seeing us off, the family members of Harish hadn't come station, as Harish was invited to speak at an LIC meeting. And it was us who convinced Ratna not to come along with us; this is how we booked an Uber and came here. On the way station one statement of Ratna, utmost bothering me, was," We had suffered severe financial turmoil after losing the case against Virendra Bhai Saheb. But as soon as I met Pranav, my thoughts sublimed. On the way back, we booked first-class tickets on the Ranchi Rajdhani Express. With a private coupe, the three of us could share our experiences. Pranav's conference had been a great success; he had a one-on-one conversation with the Home Minister and even took a selfie with him. I also learned that Srijan is running an NGO called Rural India, Real India. For a documentary on the lives of Adivasis, she would soon be visiting rural areas of Jharkhand. We felt sad that we couldn't introduce Pranav to Harish's family or meet Shavy either. Harish had come to the station to see us off if it had happened so at least Pranav could meet him but he got a sudden invitation to speak in an LIC workshop and he had to go. Srijan and Ratna wanted to come to see us off, but we insisted they didn't, so we booked an Uber and came on our own. Pranav also shared with us, "I wanted to meet Harish's uncle and Ratna's aunt, but the way this trip was planned, it just didn't happen." As soon as we reached Ranchi station, it felt as though the chapter of Delhi was slowly coming to an end—but was it so?

"

XX

FATHER CRISTOPHER PART-2

I was quite interested in Monk Philip's YouTube channel, particularly in the video of Father Christopher part 2. What hobby had I started to rear? I was getting addicted to social media. Fortunately, I found the video I had been waiting a long time for while scrolling through YouTube. I was sitting in my office and studying a case file, but my level of addiction, or you can say curiosity, shifted me from the file to YouTube without me even noticing the shift in my mind-supported act.

Monk Philip's words on the channel:

I am your friend, Philip, and you are watching "Memories of Father Christopher by Monk Philip." In this video, I highlight the lives of some people from Father's Diary who acknowledged their mistakes and sincerely tried to rectify them, serving as a source of inspiration for all of us. As you know, we do not reveal the names of individuals in this program. Today, we will draw inspiration from Mr. A once again in this show. The first part video had tremendous love from your side, for which I pay my heartfelt gratitude to all of you. The success of this show must be credited to my dear viewers and Father Christopher, who has always been a guiding pillar to all of us. Before moving forward, I want to tell everyone with folded hands that we do not intend to convert anyone to Christianity through this channel. I received many comments from people of different religions who are getting attracted to Christianity after watching it and now they want to adopt it. But I want to request all of them that all religions ultimately lead us to the same God. Religions are the only paths to reach Him, so we must stay on the path we have taken from birth. Changing paths may make your route lengthier. Now, before diving into the life of Mr A, I want to throw some light on the three parts of the mind, they are the conscious part, the subconscious part and the unconscious part. Psychologists have described that our conscious minds consist of the mental processes which are aware. The unconscious mind is the primary source of human behaviours, feelings, motives, karma etc are influenced by past experiences and stored here. The subconscious mind works tirelessly 24x7, it helps us think some something in the form of visuals, symbols, metaphors, illustrations etc. It is said that the dreams which we see while sleeping are only due to connections of some dots between unconscious and subconscious parts. To explain their interrelationship I want to share a story, or you can say a fact, with you that Father Christopher used to tell:

"Assume your brain as a three-chambered beaker, each chamber separated by semipermeable membranes. For the time being, assume that your conscious, unconscious and subconscious minds exist in liquid form. All of them are placed in the beaker being separated by the membrane. The lowest *part, i.e. unconscious part has having highest density. If the concentrations of the liquids in the three chambers of the beaker are different, there is a flow from a higher concentration to a lower one due to osmotic pressure, till the concentration of liquids in the three parts of the beaker attain equilibrium. Concentrations of liquids in the parts depend on our karmas, the liquid of the unconscious mind contains past life karma whereas the liquid of the conscious mind contains present life karmas and the subconscious mind stores the liquids from both conscious and unconscious parts depending upon variations of concentrations. If the concentration of good deeds in the unconscious part is higher, it can dilute even bad karma in the subconscious part and ultimately, the conscious part. Opposite to it, if the concentration of good karmas is higher in the conscious part, it is capable of neutralizing our past life bad karmas. The process continues until there is balance in karmic factors."*

This is the simple philosophy of karma given to us by Father Christopher. I hope everyone will understand it. Frankly speaking, it took years for me to understand.

I request you all to stay tuned until the end as this video might be lengthier.

Father Christopher wrote in his diary that Mr A had been fighting a mental battle between truth and lie for a long time. In the end, he had to leave his city and shift to another city to escape his inner turmoil, but it was not easy. He had to break the hearts of thousands of his well-wishers. Even after moving to another city, he remained connected to Father Christopher through correspondence. He had taken steps to leave behind lies, but giving up the habit of lying is as difficult as giving up the habit of alcohol. He once again succumbed to weakness and, intentionally, plunged himself into deep trouble. He put his financial and mental security, at risk to prove a point to a friend.

Once, Father Christopher explained the impact of our words and thoughts on the universe, saying, "Research has shown that every person's words are recorded in this universe, with each individual's words carrying a unique frequency, which is why they can always be distinguished. Only thoughts, words, or mantras with a high frequency can reach the Supreme Soul, while low-frequency vibrations remain at the lowest level, creating negativity in a person's life. The vibration of truth is maximum, while that of lies or manipulated words is minimal, which is why falsehood always brings sorrow and suffering."

Father's suggestions and teachings always guided Mr A in his life but sometimes it was not so smooth to stick to it and he derailed himself from the principles.

Mr A proved himself a past life close relative to his friend so that he could mould him in the manner he wished, as could win his confidence in a more easier way to motivate him. For doing it he juggled in risky ways, as he hoped God would certainly help them as there was a purity in Mr A's intentions as his friend will have success in his life in terms of getting a good job.

This step taken by him was condemned by Father Cristopher. He gave the reference to the Mahabharata, where Lord Krishna supports the trick played to kill Drona. The falsehood was shielded there because had it a wider perspective, the message that righteousness always triumphs over unrighteousness was implanted in the human mind for generations to come by Sri Krishna, who was a part of the battle of Mahabharata.

Bible's message of Jesus,' I have no greater joy than to hear that my children are walking in the truth.' God's forgiveness of telling a lie is subjective and the purpose of telling it is a key factor. A lie for one's benefit is the greatest sin and God does not forgive it, if it is spoken for the benefit of someone else or the benefit of the society as a whole, the forgiveness depends on the future course of action of the speaker.

As the Bible says,' Truthful speech has lasting quality while lies can linger self destruct', God disapproved the falsehoods which Mr A used for the sake of his friend but the best part was that he confessed in his letters to the Father, without any shame. He had written to him that to motivate his friend he extended his imaginary love cum tragic story to the next level by convincing his friend that he was his relative in his previous life,

The fluctuations of Mr A from the fine line separating truthfulness and falsehood could harm him in a deeper level of consciousness, it was the main concern of Father Cristopher. He knew that A was in a position of a pendulum which started oscillating with the help of some external force, to attain a mean position now he had to cross it several times. The Father had predicted that his illustrations of life might appear true in his life in some different form as they were getting rooted deeply in the unconscious mind which will appear in the subconscious and finally, someday start floating on the surface of the conscious mind...

The video was remaining to watch but I got the vital information I needed and at the same time Father's prediction turned out to be the cause of my worry.

After watching the video, the memory of the first case of my life surfaced in my mind. I should not have fought that case for Virendra; it was the biggest mistake of my life.

It was I who suggested Virendra lodge cases under sections 203,205 and 211 under IPC which could even damage his reputation at LIC, for God's sake, no such thing happened.

In the second and final hearing of the case, Ratna began to feel that Sudha truly existed and had been a part of

Harish's life, putting his married life at risk. Harish had assured her that there was none in his life before her 'which could prove as a void statement. Once discussions begin in court, it's hard to predict the direction they'll take. Thankfully, based on the evidence, the case took a turn, and Sudha's story was proven to be fabricated. In the story, Sudha was a fabrication so obviously it had no sense that Sudha was the past life sister of Virendra. As a result, Harish was found guilty of misleading Virendra and derailing his career, and he was ordered by the court to pay a fine

What a sarcastic, Harish was fined for derailing Virendra's career!

Today, I can see the loopholes in our judiciary system which lawyers misuse for their benefit. I still curse the day when I was convinced at Virendra's so-called pathetic situation as per his description.

XXI

RURAL INDIA- REAL INDIA

[Let's embark on a journey through rural India, specifically to the Simdega district, one of Jharkhand's 24 districts. Located in South Jharkhand, Simdega is a place where the sweet dialect of Nagpuri—a variant of Odia language known locally as Sadri—fills the air with warmth and adaptability. Rich in cultural heritage, Simdega lies in the Red Corridor and has been greatly influenced by Odia culture. Historically, it was part of the Kaisalpur-Birugarh Parganas, a kingdom ruled by the Ganga Vamsi dynasty of the Gajapati royal family, who governed for centuries, even during British colonial rule.

Simdega's development is essential for the advancement of South Jharkhand. Its close proximity to Rourkela, the industrial capital of Odisha, promises economic growth and development, benefiting the population of Southern Jharkhand.

The indigenous Sarna religion, known as "Sarna Dharma" or the "Religion of the HolyWoods(don't misunderstand it as 'Hollywoods")," is practiced by the tribal communities in Jharkhand and across the Indian subcontinent. This deep-rooted belief system is a vital part of Simdega's identity. It is said that Ram ,Laxman and Sita had been there during their exile.

Simdega is also known as the "Cradle of Hockey" in Jharkhand, having produced Olympic-level athletes who've represented India on global stages. Olympian Sylvanus Dung Dung, who won gold at the 1980 Moscow Olympics in hockey, hails from Simdega, as does Michael Kindo, an Olympian who won bronze at the 1972 Summer Olympics. Asunta Lakra, former captain of India's women's hockey team, also calls Simdega home. Recently, Simdega has welcomed an Astroturf Hockey Stadium, designed to nurture budding hockey talent from the area. Additionally, the Albert Ekka Stadium, an outdoor facility, supports other sports like football and cricket.]*

There's something special about taking you all on a journey to Simdega. It's a coincidence that Pranav is posted at Bolba police station in Simdega, and in a nearby village, Dan Gaddi, Srijan's team was coming for a documentary shoot. Since her NGO had already received permission for the documentary, from district administration, Pranav mentioned that the district office has assigned his team the responsibility of protecting Srijan and her crew. It seems that fate also agrees with what we desire as I had never discussed the name of the particular station to the family Harish , I had only told them that Pranav was posted in Simdega district.

The subject of the documentary was "The Pain of Hunger or Forest Conservation." Sushma learned from

Srijan that the theme focused on four families of the Munda community in a specific area. These families' ancestors had participated in the freedom struggle alongside Birsa Munda, yet today, their descendants live lives of hunger and humiliation. Previously, they used to cut and sell trees from the forest to make a living, but now, due to deforestation concerns, the forest department has imposed a strict ban on this activity. Anyone caught cutting trees in the forest faces severe punishment. In such a situation, how are these people supposed to feed themselves? There is no sign of any employment opportunities being provided by the government. Currently, the government provides free rice, but to cook it, they still need firewood, which is completely banned by the forest department. They don't even have money to buy salt to eat with the cooked rice. So, what are they supposed to do?

The issue seemed genuinely serious to me. Our society has many big and small issues that often go unnoticed by the common citizen. Yet it's precisely this oppressed society that, sooner or later, erupts. And then, we label it as "Naxalite" or "Lalkhandi" (leftist rebels) and hand it over to law and order without addressing the root causes. Neither the politicians nor the so-called guardians of society seem to care about such issues. Anyway, the selection of families for the documentary was done entirely by the district administration.

I felt immense pride in Srijan. Though she was just a young child, her thinking was remarkable; such thoughts could truly blossom only with the blessings of Lord Shiva.

Bringing the team from Ranchi airport and arranging their stay and meals at the Simdega Police guest house was part of my son's duty. The shooting was set to begin the next day, and it was scheduled to last a week. The first family whose home was to be featured belonged to Kaluwa Munda. Seeing the attire of the family members made one feel like crying. The men would tear a dhoti into two pieces and wear just one piece around their body, while the women wore worn-out, dirty white sarees with red borders, frayed and revealing in many places. Srijan wondered whether she should feel proud of India's greatness or weep at seeing this part of the country in the 21st century—but the truth was undeniable. Their clothing was so inadequate that there wasn't even a place to tuck the house key into their waist. One common feature found in the village was their kachcha houses with hay roofs, with bows and arrows hanging on the walls.While I was interested in the shooting itself, I was even more curious to see if their duties would sow the seeds of love and attraction between them. To keep updated on every moment, I had already enlisted Pranav's constable, Jagdip Mahto, for information. If they missed the opportunities that fate had placed in their lives, it would have been deeply disappointing for me.

The week-long shoot had concluded, and Srijan's team had returned to Delhi, but Pranav hadn't shared any updates about Srijan with his mother. As for him informing me, that was out of the question. However, three photos from Jagdeep Mahto gave me a glimmer of hope, showing clear closeness between them. The photos were taken near the Dan Gaddi waterfall, close to the Ban Durga temple, and around the Ramrekha Dham area. I really liked these photos, with Pranav dressed in civilian attire, and I must have shown them to Sushma countless times. Sushma, too, was optimistic, but finally, giving in to my antics, she asked me to share the photos with her on her phone, which I did.

We left everything on Durga Mata and Bhagwan Sri Ram.

Sushma had told Pranav over the phone to take three or four days' leave and come to Namkum so she could understand what was on his mind, as not everything can be discussed over the phone. But his response was, "No, Mom, it's absolutely impossible to come to Namkum until the election in two months. After that, I'll come and stay for 10-15 days. We'll go out, travel, and spend time together."

Yes, exactly; during election time, the workload of the police department increases significantly, and this time the Simdega election is quite special. It's notable because only three candidates are running in this constituency. The first is Ram Khelawan Singh, a well-known leader from a national party. The second is Dukhna Oraon, an independent candidate, and the third candidate is Surekha Bai from the JAL (Jharkhand Awami League) party, who is from the transgender community. Her party is a regional one. There is fierce competition among all three candidates.

I don't possess divine vision like Sanjay from the Mahabharata, yet I remain aware of all the political activities happening across Jharkhand. I know what's going on at every moment—perhaps because I am a lawyer.

Only a few days had passed, and election campaigning was at its peak. The Simdega election was particularly notable, as Ram Khilawan Singh was a powerful, seasoned leader with considerable influence and the backing of a major party. On the other hand, Surekha Bai, being a transgender candidate, could attract a large sympathy vote, although she was new to the world of politics. However, recent reform steps taken by the Home Minister for the transgender community could benefit Surekha Ji a lot.

Dukhna Oraon, could significantly split the votes between the other two candidates. Considering Jharkhand's caste dynamics, it can be said that he could secure a substantial share of votes from the Oraons, Kharias, Mundas, Asurs, and Birhors. Although these communities together make up about 80 percent of the electorate, Dukhna Ji's criminal background led to some controversy during his nomination filing, causing him to lose some credibility; otherwise, he would also have been in the race for victory. His independent candidature was also a drawback for him.

With just a week left in the election, the shocking news of Dukhna Oraon's murder had caused an upheaval in the political corridors of Jharkhand. Suspicion pointed towards Surekha ji. No one was found at the scene of the incident. Dukhna ji's body was cremated with full honors, and on this occasion, Ram Khilawan ji was present. While giving an interview to the Awaz newspaper, he said, "Undoubtedly, this is the work of our opponents. In the pursuit of political gain, we have lost a great leader. I will request the police and administration to identify the murderer as soon as possible and put him behind bars."

The Election Commission canceled the Simdega election. Based on suspicion, Surekha Bai was arrested, and the police also took Kaluwa Munda's into custody due to the recovery of a homemade pistol from his house.

In the police investigation, it was found that Dukhna Munda was killed with the same pistol, and the actual owner of this pistol was revealed to be Surekha Bai, who was eventually jailed. Surekha Ji's people appealed in the Ranchi High Court, and S R Associates was going to fight this case. I don't know how this case came to our firm, but this time, Jannie expressed a desire to plead the case. Recognizing her talent, I gave her permission to handle it. Jannie herself, along with Gaurang, went to Simdega to gather details and evidence for the case. She took Pranav's full assistance in this process, and Srijan's documentary film proved to be very useful.

Hearing of Surekha Bai Case:

In this case, the judge's seat was held by Prahlad Tiwari, and the government prosecutor was Advocate Jugnoo Gogoi, who was part of Shyam Jalani's team. Today my presence in the court was just as a spectator.

As soon as Mr. Tiwari entered the courtroom, a hush fell over the room. Just moments before, there had been a strange uproar. Voices echoed, with some saying, "These kinnars have no morality ," while others murmured, "If such people are sent to parliament, who knows where the country will go," and various other comments. But now, everyone stood respectfully, giving due regard to the judge. Judge Prahlad instructed, "Everyone, please be seated, and Mr. Gogoi, present the details of the case so proceedings may continue."

Advocate Gogoi, while handing over a file of documents, said, "Thank you, my Lord. This case involves a heinous act driven by political motives. For her own political gain, Surekha Bai hired Kaluwa Munda to kill her independent election rival, Mr. Dukhna Oraon, hoping to secure a portion of his votes. The pistol recovered from Kaluwa's house, along with his admission that he was hired by Surekha, are clear indications of her involvement in this crime. Therefore, it is an open-and-shut case. I respectfully request, my Lord, that Surekha be given such a severe punishment that it serves as a deterrent to others who might consider committing similar crimes in the future."

Advocate Jannie stood in a furry and said," I object my Lord, my friend is in a great hurry to declare the result of the case, he has forgotten that we here to challenge the verdict of the sub-ordinate court and discuss the pros and cons of it in a fresh way."

Suddenly, when my gaze fell upon Surekha Bai, I felt like I had seen her somewhere before, but where? I couldn't recall. Just outside the courtroom, when I had a word with Judge Tiwari, he had jokingly said, "Have you retired? Today, your assistant Jannie is pleading the case." I brushed off his comment, saying it was nothing like that. But the way my memory was playing tricks on me made me feel that maybe it was time to retire from law. I was lost in these thoughts when a significant part of the court proceedings had already moved forward. Jannie had called her witness, Jiwadhan Mahto, to the stand and had started questioning him, finally snapping me back to attention.

Jannie said to Jiwadhan," Please introduce yourself to the court, and describe whatever you know about the case"

Jiwadhan answered," My Lord, my name is Jiwadhan Mahto, I work as head clerk in the Dan Daga block office, I good hold at regional languages spoken in this locality as I have to come across a number of people speaking Nagpuri, Mundari, Oria etc, daily apart from it I am good at Hindi and English. A month ago an NGO team named Rural India,Real India had come in our panchayat for shooting documentary film, the team members were facing problems in speaking regional languages so our BDO had deputed me as the translator of the team."

Jannie- Come to your linkings to the case.

Jiwadhan- "To find my linking to the case is not as important as to investigate the linkings of others as finding something important regarding the case the court should listen to facts which I had observed during the shoot:

Fact 1: One day during the shoot Kameshwar Singh entered the house of Kaluwa, he was unaware that he was in the range of the camera shoot, gave a pouch containing something hard and Kaluwa put it into the quiver.

Fact 2: In the interview, Kaluwa shared that his wife had passed away years ago during the birth of their youngest daughter, leaving behind two small children. She departed from this world, taking along one of her cherished desires—her love for wearing gold earrings. In this community, due to the grip of poverty, no one can afford gold, so they fulfil their wishes by wearing jewellery made of brass instead. But his wife had a deep fondness for gold earrings nonetheless. Almost every night since her death, she appears in Kaluwa's dreams, asking him to buy gold earrings for their daughter. He loves his wife dearly, but due to their poverty, he's unable to buy gold

Fact 3: He had promised her wife never to tell a lie.

Fact 4: On the last day of the shoot I saw both of his daughters wearing golden rings. My lord now court can link all the facts to reach some valid conclusion"

Mr Gogoi said in a furious mood," My Lord Ms Jannie is misleading the court with the absurd story."

Ms Jannie said," No story is absurd here, my Lord, I seek your permission to call Mr Kameshwar Singh in the witness box."

Judge- Permission granted

Jannie(from Kameshwar in the witness box)-Tell your name and your relationship with MP contestant Mr Ram Khilawan Singh.

Kameshwar- My Lord, I am Kameshwar Singh and I am the younger brother of Mr Ram Khilawan Singh.

Jannie-Tell what object had you given to Kaluwa in the pouch, a day before the murder of Dukhna Oraon. (she warned that everything was shot into the camera and they knew everything, She said that she had sent already the videos to Judge Saheb, and I want your confirmation that might be the cause of your exemption from punishment.)

Kameshwar(with fear and hesitation)-They were golden rings for Kaluwa's daughters.

Jannie- Then, are you sure, you haven't given a pistol to him on that day ?

Kameshwar-Yes sure.

Jannie-How can you say it?

Kameshwar(hurriedly)-I had given that to him a week ago.

After speaking he was amazed, what had he spoken!

Jannie told the court," My Lord, if golden rings are given in pouch, no video can take the photos of rings and giving the pistol to Kaluwa was just my guess and he accepted his act. Now Kameshwar will explain everything if the court guarantees him to announce government witness to get relief from punishment.

Before recording Rameshwar's statement she called Kaluwa along with the translator Jiwadhan. Kaluwa gave statements in Nagpuri which was translated in Hindi by Jiwadhan.

He was persuaded to tell the truth by invoking the memory of his deceased wife, and he became emotional, revealing the whole story. He admitted that he shot Dukhna to get gold rings for his children and informed the police that the pistol he used to kill was provided to him by Surekha Ji. Rameshwar Ji had orchestrated circumstances in such a way that suspicion would fall on Dukhna. In the subordinate court, it was mentioned that this pistol belonged to Surekha, which is indeed true. When she was the head of the transgender community, she acquired this weapon for protection. Though it was an illegal then, homemade gun, she had legalized it by paying a penalty at the police station. She had also reported its theft from her home to the police but had kept it confidential. Kameshwar took advantage of these events, which ultimately led the pistol to reach Kaluwa

In the end, Kameshwar confessed that all plotting was a part of a conspiracy of Ram Khilawan Bhaiya and how he arranged for a man to steal Surekha's pistol from one of her own employees.

Before Judge Tiwari, could read the verdict, I was simply hypnotised by the ways Jannie pleaded the case and I thought I had got my heir for S.R. Associates. ,I could not even smell how she collected clues , how she used Jiwadhan's intellect, of course in all these Pranav had just been played a vital role and I can't forget the contributions of Gourang.

Meanwhile, the verdict by Mr Tiwari drew my attention,".....Kaluwa is given four years jail for killing Dukhna Oraon,...Surekha Bai is made free from all her allegations and the court feels sorry for making her victim

of the great conspiracy." Court had issued a warrant to arrest Ram Khilawan Singh and

an illegal lawsuit should be filed."

Jannie went to Surekha Bai, touched her feet, and said,"Now, aunt, no one can defeat you in the by-election."

Of a sudden I almost recalled her, she was definitely, the one who had rescued Jannie from the dustbin. They both came to me, I was amazed to see them together. She said,

"Sir, please don't be surprised at all. I've been in touch with Surekha Aunty for quite some time. Sir, I'm your student after all. You may have a reputation for secrecy, but you had hidden some big secrets yourself, so I felt it was my place to dig deeper. When we went to Doranda police station for the state government survey, you got upset after gathering some information, left all the work to Gourang, and searched for something. When I heard from Gourang about your distress, I got involved, and you know I don't stop until I find out what I want to know. I discovered all the secrets you had hidden in your heart for years. When Surekha Aunty got caught up with Ram Kilawan, her people consulted me, and that's how this case came to our firm—one that wasn't a rape case."

I had no words. I only said," Have you told all these to DeSouzas?"

She said," Please don't worry, they are my parents and parents forever."

XXII
DESTITY'S DECISION

Last night, Harish called me, as promised. Our conversation lasted nearly 45 minutes, and he seemed calm and patient, though it was clear that destiny had taken an unexpected turn in his life. He was waiting for the hand of fate to play its next move. What struck me was how his imaginary tale seemed to manifest itself in his son's life, Shavy. Harish's long-standing habit of telling lies had tragically affected Shavy, who had come from Texas to confront unresolved issues from his past.

Before diving into these unresolved matters—long buried in Shavy's unconscious mind and now rising to the surface—I found myself comparing two love stories I had heard years ago and the one Harish recounted to me last night.

Harish's Past Life Love Story:
Authenticity: Fake/Imaginary
Central Figure: Sudha

Hobby: Singing

Family Status: Mother deceased

First Sight of Love: Patliputra Medical College

First Meeting: Dhanbad Railway Station, Platform No. 4

End: Sudha was abducted and killed

Twists and Turns: Sudha appears in Harish's dreams as a guide after death.

Posthumous Responsibility: Sudha assigned Harish the task of making Virendra financially successful.

Shavy's Recent Love Story:

Authenticity: True/Innocent

Central Figure: Aurelia

Hobby: Playing the ukulele

Family Status: Raised by her mother after a divorce

First Sight of Love: Music Concert

First Meeting: Texas Airport, Terminal 4

End: Aurelia was killed in a terrorist attack.

Twists and Turns: After death, Aurelia appears in Shavy's dreams as a past and future guide.

Posthumous Responsibility: Aurelia entrusted Shavy with the task of finding their past-life daughter, who is currently in crisis.

The Story as Revealed by Harish:

Shavy had been working as senior consultant at the IT solutions company Cognitive Scales in Texas when he first encountered Aurelia, a Texas University student, during a concert. Aurelia, a talented ukulele player and a member of the Mad Angle Music Band, captivated Shavy. Her father, a Pakistani, had divorced her mother over a minor issue, leaving her mother to raise Aurelia alone in the United States.

Shavy and Aurelia met for the first time at Texas International Airport, Terminal 4. Their flights had been delayed due to bad weather, giving them hours to talk. They discussed their hobbies and shared personal stories, and they were deeply connected by the time they departed. In each other's absence, they felt a growing emptiness in their hearts—an unmistakable sign that love had begun to blossom.

But fate had other plans. In June 2016, during Pride Month, the United States experienced the deadliest mass shooting in its history at the Pulse gay nightclub in Orlando, where 49 people were killed. Although security forces had issued warnings of similar attacks in 2024, several incidents still occurred, targeting the LGBT+ community across various cities. The Mad Angle Band, which included many LGBT artists, became a victim as well. Tragically, Aurelia and two other musicians lost their lives in one such attack, leaving Shavy heartbroken and alone in a foreign land.

During this painful time, Shavy confided in his sister, Srijan, sharing the depth of his sorrow. Yet Harish could barely comprehend the extent of his son's pain.

The Past Life Agenda:

After her death, Aurelia began appearing in Shavy's dreams. She gave him several tasks:

1)Apply for a job transfer to Cognitive Corporate Solutions in Gurugram, Haryana, India.

2)Befriend Salma Khatoon, a strategic consultant at the office.

3)Investigate Salma's connection to Rukhsana, a transgender woman living in Saharanpur, U.P.

4)Legally secure the release of a two-year-old girl, Rubbaiya, from Rukhsana's custody.

5)Adopt Rubbaiya, their past-life daughter, and raise her in this life.

The mention of Salma Khatoon during my conversation with Harish sparked a flurry of connections in my mind I have got the answer to questions that Prakash had left unanswered at Beguluru. Suddenly, everything became clear—not just about Shavy, but also about Nitin's past love life at the Gopalan Florenza Apartments in Bengaluru.

However, one statement from Harish still weighed heavily on me: "My lies have ruined my children's lives. Both Shavy and Srijan are trapped in their traumas."

I, too, spent many sleepless nights, haunted by the question: Were my friend's habitual and helpless-intentional, lies responsible for Shavy and Srijan's suffering?

Months later, Harish called me again. This time, his voice brimmed with confidence and relief. "Raaj, my friend," he said, "I can finally die in peace. The grace of the Almighty has resolved everything. I now have my granddaughter, Rubbaiya, in my life. Shavy has formed a strong friendship with Salma, and as for Srijan, Sarvesh Bhaiya's friend, Dr Lethabo, from the U.S., has discovered a cure for her illness.', we are very hopeful"

It seemed that the slate had finally been wiped clean. On the unconscious mind, a whiteboard appeared, with no deposition of 'Prarabdha' in it.

His sense of relief, how I could even explain it, brought me such comfort. Suddenly, I felt as if I had stepped out of my domain of guilt.

I had started to feel a slight change in my perspective on life. Life now felt less like a stage and more like a courtroom. An invisible judge, with ourselves as our own lawyer... the verdict inevitable... justice certain, regardless of whether any court in the world delivered justice or denied it ,punishment for a wrong act awarded or not .

I am simple Rajesh Mathur now, no R..A..A..J, I don't like mysteries any more in my life except that of the birth of Jannie, after all, she has given the real meaning to De Souza's life.

Epilogue

The story of the novel 'Fake Calls Of Destiny' does not conclude neatly, tied up with answers or resolutions. Life rarely offers us such clarity. As the years pass and the dust of their struggles settles, what remains is not their triumphs or failures but the echoes of the choices they made—the truths they lived by and the lies they carried to protect or destroy one another. The calls of destiny sometimes seem fake but they seem original with the other angle.

Harish's death left a void, not only in the lives of his family members and those who knew him but in the very fabric of his existence. A few days before his death, Harish's late mother appeared to him in a dream. She said, "Son, I could never openly express my love for you while I was alive. The atmosphere at home and your father's excessive inclination toward Sarvesh compelled me to remain a devoted wife and support him. I could never think about you. Son, come to me now, into my embrace."

Ratna sometimes trembles with fear, wondering, "Did I end up torturing Harish in the name of truth and clarity?.. If it is thought this way, I too kept Harish in the dark—I never mentioned my school-life crush, Jiwan, to him. Now, sometimes I had been feeling my principles, hollow."How wonderful it would be if, before expecting to see a virtue in someone else, we first ensured that the same virtue exists within us? In the words of Gandhi Ji, "If you want to change the world, start with yourself." Yet, in the family, Rubbaiya had risen to embody the very essence of her grandfather and had become her grandmother's best friend. The inspirational and motivational thoughts of Harish will continue to energize many in LIC. to work, with exceptional zeal.

The LIC can never forget Harish's contribution. In life, no one's place remains empty, but perhaps no one can ever take Harish's place. His life, a quiet testament to sacrifice, loyalty, and regret, stands as a reminder of the perilous path of compromise. Though Harish passed with accusations he never deserved, his ultimate acceptance of the unyielding power of truth—Satyam Shivam Sundaram—offers a glimmer of redemption. His heart, burdened with the weight of his actions and inactions, found peace in the understanding that truth, no matter how long obscured, is the final arbiter. Virendra, ever the enigma, remains a symbol of ambition without bounds. His victories in the business world echo hollow in his soul's chambers. As the twilight of his life looms, the realization dawns that the cost of his cunning was not merely his conscience but the hearts he left scarred in his wake. He stands as a monument to the dual-edged nature of success—a cautionary tale for those who would sacrifice their moral compass for power and wealth. Virendra's selfish motives and relentless chase for money, without concern for right or wrong, truth or lies, shaped Harish's personality. They pushed him to become a newer and better version of himself daily. It is said that Ravana's contribution to making Ram the epitome of virtue, Maryada Purushottam, was unparalleled.

Raaj, the voice that carried us through this tale, discontinues his work as a lawyer, leaving S R Associates, in the right hand of Jannie—a seeker of justice in a world often devoid of it. Raaj's journey is one of quiet introspection, of wrestling with the complexities of human relationships and the burdens of truth. He emerges not as a man with all the answers but as one who understands the value of questions about loyalty, love, and the fine line between truth and lies. Through Raaj, the story invites us to look inward, confront the uncomfortable truths of our own lives, and embrace humanity's messy, imperfect beauty.

The story of these three men is not just theirs; it is ours. It is the story of a world grappling with the evolving definitions of morality, the shifting sands of loyalty, and the truths we bury beneath layers of lies. Through the tangled threads of their lives, we see reflections of our struggles, hopes, and failures. As the final pages close, the lessons linger: Truth, though often painful, is the foundation of all that is good. Love, though fragile, is the anchor that holds us steady. Sacrifice, though costly, is the bridge to redemption. May we all find the courage to live by these truths, however imperfectly, and to seek the balance between ambition, love, and the ultimate pursuit of a life well lived. The story of the three friends is over, but its echoes remain. They remind us that life is not about the resolutions we achieve but the questions we dare to ask and the truths we strive to uphold.

In the end, I believe this: within each of us lies a part of Virendra and a part of Raaj—or Raadaan. It's up to us to decide how much room we allow each to occupy. Do we nurture the innocence of Rubbaiya, the creative spirit of Srijan, or the heartfelt emotions of Pranav? Can we reflect on the struggles of the LGBTQA community and their fight for acceptance? Do we honour the sacrifices of Shavy, embrace the forgiveness of Nitin, or cultivate a deep understanding of Andy? The answers shape not just who we are, but the world we leave behind.